Entropia

Samuel Alexander

ENTROPIA: LIFE BEYOND INDUSTRIAL CIVILISATION

First published by the Simplicity Institute, Melbourne, 2013

www.simplicityinstitute.org

Cover and map design by Andrew Doodson © 2013

ISBN-13: 978-0-9875884-0-1

Disclaimer: Entropia, in the English language, is an invented word that has been used occasionally in academic contexts and commercially. In this book the author uses the word independently and descriptively, claiming no association with any other uses or entities.

Entropia is a masterful work of the imagination that envisions a world beyond growth and consumerism. This is no escapist fantasy, however, but rather a practical and inspiring reminder of what we humans are capable of – and a wake up call to action. It is a literary manifesto that will inspire, challenge, and give hope."

Paul Gilding, *The Great Disruption*

"Looking back from the future, this visionary book describes the emergence of a culture and economy based on material sufficiency. In doing so it provides one of the most detailed descriptions we have of an ecologically sane way of life. Overflowing with insight and beautifully written, *Entropia* unveils the radical implications of moving beyond fossil fuels. This book may come to define what 'sustainability' really means."

Richard Heinberg, *The End of Growth*

"Utopian novels usually outline a world of material abundance, in which technology has reduced labour to a minimum and where everyone is rich. But Samuel Alexander, following the tradition of Henry Thoreau and William Morris, has written a 'utopia of sufficiency', in which a simple living community of poet-farmers rebuild their society after the collapse of civilisation. *Entropia* is both confronting and inspiring, giving us an insight into the possibility of a much saner and more satisfying world."

Ted Trainer, *Transition to a Sustainable and Just World*

"One of the more intriguing attempts to date to imagine a viable future on the far side of our civilisation's decline and fall, Samuel Alexander's *Entropia* borrows the language of Utopian literature to present alternative visions of politics, society, and spirituality in the aftermath of the industrial age."

John Michael Greer, *The Ecotechnic Future: Envisioning a Post-Peak World*

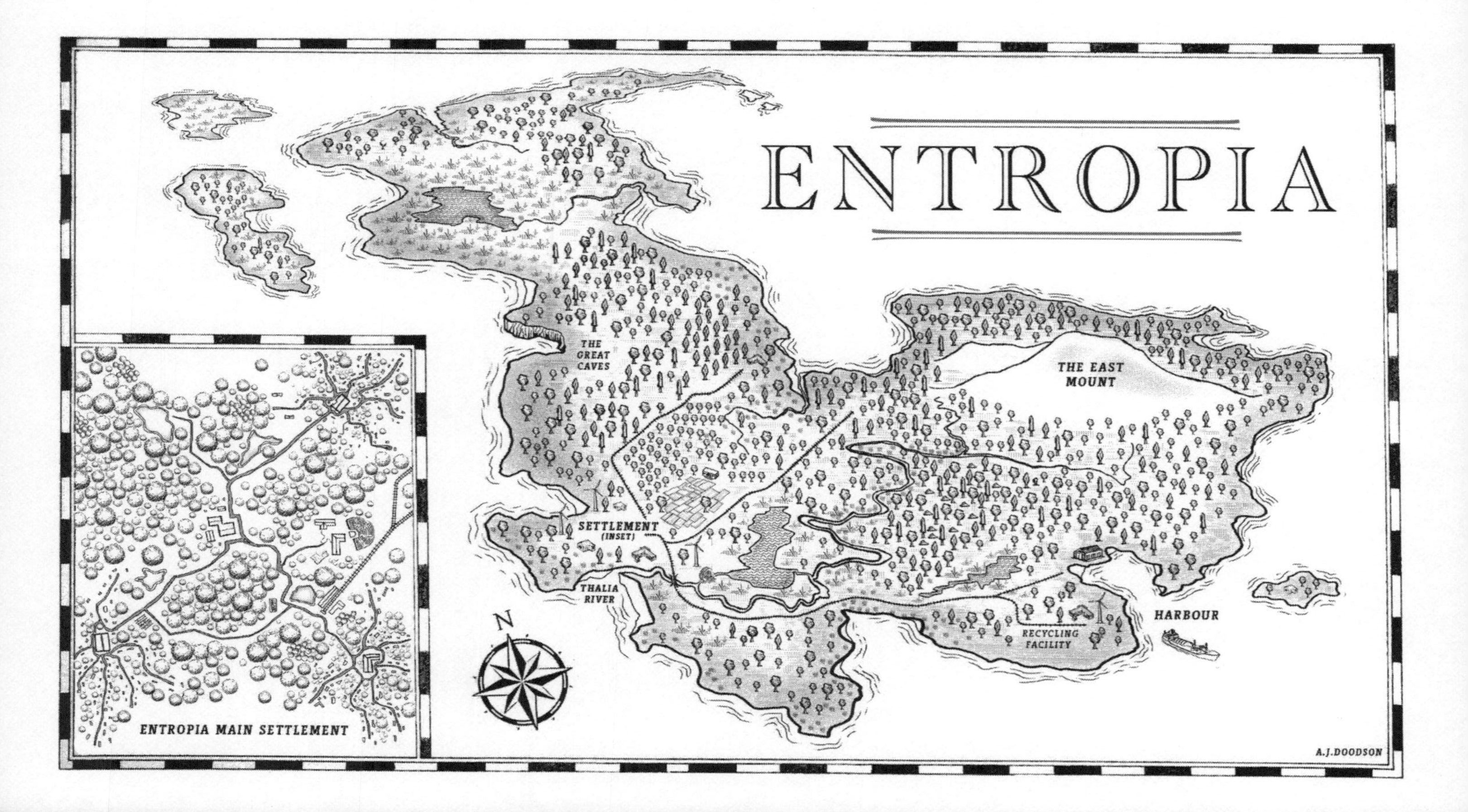
ENTROPIA
THE GREAT CAVES
THE EAST MOUNT
SETTLEMENT (INSET)
THALIA RIVER
RECYCLING FACILITY
HARBOUR
N
ENTROPIA MAIN SETTLEMENT
A.J.DOODSON

CONTENTS

Acknowledgements

In writing this 'utopia of sufficiency' I was influenced and inspired by many people. Henry Thoreau has been by far the greatest influence on my worldview, for it was he who awakened me to the insight that 'superfluous wealth can buy superfluities only'. It is easy to forget that insight, however, and fall back to sleep, so in order to negotiate the path of sufficiency successfully, I discovered that it is essential to practise techniques of mindfulness and self-discipline, a lesson I learnt first from the Greek and Roman Stoics. William Morris, in his utopian novel, *News from Nowhere*, helped me to see what a society based on material sufficiency might look like, and John Stuart Mill taught me that a time would come when a stationary, non-growing economy would be not just socially desirable but ecologically necessary. Consequently, the best ideas in the following pages are already expressed in the works of these great thinkers and writers, so if there is any originality to the message my book delivers, it is only through synthesising those ideas and creatively adapting them to very different times.

I am also greatly indebted to my colleagues and fellow authors at the Simplicity Institute – Ted Trainer, Mark Burch, David Holmgren, and Simon Ussher – all of whom, in their own way, have deeply shaped the social vision presented in this book. Additionally, I must acknowledge Serge Latouche, whose work introduced me to the insight that 'degrowth', not merely zero-growth, is what is needed to achieve sustainability in overdeveloped nations. With respect to energy, Howard and Elisabeth Odum and Joseph Tainter have been my biggest influences, showing me how central energy is to the world we live in. Finally, I must acknowledge Rob Hopkins and the Transition Movement, for developing what I consider to be the most promising framework for bringing about a just and sustainable, post-carbon world.

Many people read drafts of this book and discussed them with me. I would like to thank Michael Green, Andy Gibson, Helen Duckham, Johnny Rutherford, Imogen Jubb, Martin Hanson, Katherine Copsey, Aaron Brenneman, Clare Kirk, and Mark Burch, for offering me such helpful feedback and some vital encouragement. I owe special thanks to Andrew 'the wizard' Doodson, for designing the perfect cover and map; Merridy Pugh, for proofreading the manuscript; and Derek Baron for assisting me with online publication. I am lucky to have such amazing friends.

I dedicate this book to Helen and Laurie, for showing me how beautiful life can be when living simply, laughing often, and loving deeply.

Prologue

After the poets were banished from Plato's Republic it is said that they set sail into unknown horizons in search of a new place to call home. They had come to the conclusion that being accepted in such a civilisation was not a prize worth fighting for, so they chose not to resist their violent eviction and just left civilisation to itself, liberating themselves from its curse in the process. No matter how heavy the burden of freedom might be, the poets knew that the burden would always be preferable to the chains from which it arose.

For months the poets searched for new lands, often in raging seas, exploring the vast blue yonder with hopeful determination. But, alas, all their efforts met with no success. As food supplies diminished, and finding the oceans empty, hopes of survival began to fade. One poet even expressed the grim judgment that their collective existence would soon expire, and in silence they all began meditating on this imminent and seemingly unavoidable reality with stoic resignation. That fateful night, as the poets were on the brink of starvation, the seas raged higher than ever before, thunder roared fiercely and lighting crashed, and in the darkness it seemed as if their story was in fact in its closing chapter. Looking death in the face, the poets began chanting their own requiem in a state of passionate tranquillity – '*Amor fati! Amor fati!*' – accompanied in the background by Nature's primal scream. As the waves reached upward into the infinite abyss, it seemed their story was complete.

But life proceeds in twists and turns, not straight lines. After losing consciousness in the midst of this perfect storm, the lost poets found themselves washed ashore on a small, fertile island, which was uninhabited and isolated entirely from the rest of civilisation. The boundless opportunities presented by this merciful twist of fate were immediately clear to all. Far from being complete, it seemed their story was just beginning! The poets subsisted for a short time on whatever they could find, roaming the island's forests and meadows in search of food, drinking from its rivers and ponds, and sleeping in caves. But before long they settled as subsistence farmers and began building a New World according to their own poetic conception of life. They had been given what was essentially a blank canvas and were determined to live the life they had imagined. It was their duty as well as their destiny.

Determined above all else to transcend the materialistic values of the Old World, the members of this unique poetic community made a commitment early on to live materially simple lives, convinced that this was the surest path to genuine freedom, peace, and prosperity. The poets thus dedicated their time and energy not to the endless pursuit of material riches, fine clothing, or extravagant architecture, but to exploring the simple but infinite joys of nature, society, gardening, sensuality, spiritual exploration, and uninhibited creative activity – especially writing, craft, and music. It was in this very simplicity of living that they discovered a new consciousness and an unimagined existential wealth. Life was universally affirmed by these poet-farmers, and for the first and only time in human history the distinction between art and life blurred to vanishing point. This was truly a Golden Age in the human story – the peak of civilisation.

Some people believe this simple living community flourishes peacefully to this day, lost to the world in its own harmonious, aesthetic existence. But like Atlantis, the Isle of

Furor Poeticus, as it has come to be known, has never been found.

♦ ♦ ♦

The Isle of Furor Poeticus is a utopian romance of course – a myth. But we should remember that human existence has always been shaped and guided by myths and stories, so let us not dismiss the story of the lost poets too quickly or proudly. After all, we may not be so free from superstitions of our own. Modernity's 'myth of progress' might itself just be a story we have been telling ourselves in recent centuries, one in fact that could soon be dismissed as a story no longer worth telling. Indeed, perhaps that book is closing before our very eyes – has already closed – leaving us to reflect on its themes from beyond as we step forth into unknown pages. And yet, it seems we have not found a new story by which to live. We are the generation in-between stories, desperately clinging to yesterday's story but uncertain of tomorrow's. Adrift in the cosmos, without a narrative in which to lay down new roots, humanity marches on – lost and directionless. But then again, perhaps the new words we need are already with us. Perhaps we just need to live them into existence.

♦ ♦ ♦

Human beings are story-telling creatures. This has always been so. We tell each other stories to ask and explore the question of what it means to be human, even though we usually discover that the answer lies simply in the questioning itself. Every individual life and every society is an enactment of a story people tell themselves about the nature and purpose of their existence and of the world they live in. The myths we tell ourselves shape our perception of the present and guide us as we move into the future, influencing our interpretations of what is possible, proper, and important. Operating most of the time beneath the level of consciousness, myths define the contours of the human situation and the human condition, placing us in the cosmos and structuring our identities. As poetic phenomena, myths are both the centre and the circumference of our Being.

It would seem to be of some importance, therefore, to expose and understand the myths that dominate the present, so far as that is possible, while also trying to envision what life would be like, or could be like, if we were to liberate ourselves from today's myths and step into new myths. Unfortunately, however, our myths today have become so entrenched that they have assumed a false necessity, which is to say, they no longer seem to be myths at all. Rather, the myths of industrial civilisation – which are the myths of growth, technology, and affluence – seem to be a reflection of some brute laws of history from which we cannot escape. This tempts us to submit to the existing order of things, and surrender to its dictates, as if there were no alternative paths to follow or create. But we could free ourselves from this bondage of the mind, and free ourselves from ourselves in the process, if only in a moment of madness we dared to plunge into the icy waters of introspection and shake ourselves awake. By choosing to do so we could again become the poets of our own lives and of a new generation, instead of merely reading out a pre-written script to an audience that is no longer listening. So open your mind, gentle reader, for the future is but clay in the hands of our imaginations.

We are being called to make things new.

If you have built castles in the air, your work need not be lost; that is where they should be. Now put the foundations under them.

HENRY DAVID THOREAU

1

Castles in the Air

The story I am to tell you in this book is a story about a community that became isolated on its small island in the wake of industrial civilisation's collapse, during the third decade of the twenty-first century. Those who grew up on the Isle, as I did, sometimes liked to jest that we were the descendents of Plato's banished poets, but the reality is that our humble story is considerably less romantic, with more grit and tears than any fairy tale could ever allow. Still, without false modesty, it can be said that there are certain similarities between our story and the story of Plato's poets, and it is those similarities that have prompted me, seven decades after the Great Disruption, to put our unfinished story into words. Admittedly, it may seem presumptuous of me to tell this tale, for I cannot claim to have any special insight into our way of life, other than the insight gained from being an ordinary member of my community. But perhaps that very ordinariness is what makes me a suitable guide. Whatever the case, the following account is motivated only by my desire to describe the nature of our way of life openly and accurately, as it has taken form in this final year of the twenty-first century. While I am convinced that this tale deserves to be told – if only to give account of an unusual and remarkable form of life – readers who are not curious to know more need read no further, bearing in mind only that for them this book was not written.

♦ ♦ ♦

The story begins, somewhat unexpectedly no doubt, with a Texan oil magnate named Mortimer Flynn. The only child of a successful coal industrialist in Wales, Flynn sailed to the Americas in 1913 in search of wealth and adventure, hoping that the skills from his Oxford studies in economics and mechanical engineering would be in high demand in those regions where oil production was fast expanding. As things turned out, his hopes were not disappointed. Before long he had made a name for himself in the industry, and the business acumen that he developed left him eager to exploit his keen eye for investment. When his parents died in a train accident in 1919, leaving Mortimer a considerable inheritance, he found himself with the capital he needed for what eventually became the largest oil production company in Texas – Flynn and Co. A result of hard work, a small amount of luck, and an untroubled proclivity toward under-handed business practices, by the time Mortimer Flynn was forty he had become one of the richest and most powerful men in America.

By any conventional standard, Flynn was living a supremely successful life of the highest distinction. His oil empire proudly cast long shadows across the continent, and vast though it was, his empire continued to expand without any sign of letting up, driven onward by Flynn's ravenous ambition. His friends admired him, his enemies feared him, and his name became known throughout the world, all of which gave Flynn considerable satisfaction. The enormous wealth that he had accumulated even placed in his hands what seemed like godly power, for he had discovered that there was very little in life that his persuasive chequebook could not either acquire or remove, directly or indirectly, justly or unjustly. Even the politicians were in his pockets, eager to indulge his every whim in the hope of favour or reward. All this allowed Flynn to carry himself with an unaffected confidence that seemed almost majestic. In short, he always looked in control.

Perhaps owing to his power, Flynn's life also seemed to be characterised by pleasure and what one might even call happiness. Despite being cold and austere in his business practices, Flynn enjoyed a luxurious personal life of unbridled extravagance, and for this he became even more notorious than he was as a ruthless and astute businessman. His lavish and exclusive soirees were always the talk of the times, as he would invite his guests to one of his mansions, sometimes for days or even weeks on end, and shower them with expensive gifts, the most exotic foods, and the finest entertainment money could buy. In addition to all this fame, luxury, and power, Flynn had a beautiful young wife, with whom he had two healthy children, and in this family life he seemed perfectly happy and content. Without exaggeration it can be said that Mortimer Flynn had achieved everything of which he had ever dreamed, and indeed so much more. He was truly a rare event, a spectacle of worldly success.

♦ ♦ ♦

But gold does not always glitter – and achieving one's dreams will not quench the fire in one's belly if it turns out that those dreams were misconceived. Perhaps Flynn always had doubts about the authenticity of his life's direction, forever suspecting in the depths of his nature that they were really his father's dreams, or, more accurately, the world's dreams, which he had unthinkingly adopted as his own out of some cowardly need to conform. But for some years he had repressed that suspicion or dismissed it prematurely as merely the unyielding ache of youth. As his wealth and power began to grow, however, that strange ache intensified and began to crescendo, developing into something clearer and much more frightening. Flynn began questioning the real end towards which all his vital energies were directed, and this inquiry gave rise to an acute anxiety deep in his gut, which began to manifest in his life in the form of frequent outbursts of rage, often prompted by the smallest annoyances or distractions.

During one dark night of the soul, as he meditated on the meaning of his life in a cold sweat, Flynn realised that absolutely nothing – no reason for being – lay at the foundation of his existence. As he looked at himself in the mirror, he was aghast to discover that he could not even answer the question of what his oil empire was *for*. Who, then, was Mortimer Flynn? This question shattered the mirror into which he stared. He realised all at once that he had been running in the ruts of life with no conscious purpose, with no end to justify all his labours. Now that he had achieved all that he been aiming for, he saw himself for what he was – a pretentious fool, a hollow man.

His entire value system, in which he had felt so safe and secure, was suddenly turned upside down and inside out, causing Flynn to experience a profound crisis of conscience from which he would never fully recover. His every success now seemed to him empty and pointless, his highest ideals testament only to a chronic failure of imagination. Bedridden for several months by what his doctor called a 'breakdown of the nervous system', Flynn knew that something much more significant had occurred.

He had woken up to his life of bad faith.

♦ ♦ ♦

Months passed without any outward sign of improvement in Flynn's condition, and his doctor had even come to think that there would be no recovery. One morning, however, without any warning or explanation, Flynn's extended period of isolation in the darkness of his bedroom came to an abrupt end. He rose from his bed, drew his curtains, took a long, hot bath, and after getting into one of his suits, promptly resumed his formal duties at the head of his oil company, as if nothing had changed. Everything *had* changed, of course, and Flynn was simply adjusting to the bright light of his new reality before deciding on, or acting out, his next move. As if it were a play, the world watched on with bated breath.

In his absence, Flynn and Co had been managed competently though conservatively by its board of directors, which was instructed at once to give Flynn a thorough briefing on all that had happened in the months since his breakdown. The board interpreted this positively, as a sign that the old Flynn had returned to lead the company once again as meticulously and boldly as he had done in the past. After a few short weeks, however, just as Flynn became fully versed in the existing state of his company and of the oil markets more generally, he made a public announcement that would astonish and confuse not just the board of directors, but the entire world. At a press conference in New York, on 3 March 1932, Flynn announced that he had sold every share in his company and was resigning as its managing director, effective immediately. His only further comment was that he was leaving the world of business forever to pursue 'other interests' with his family, in some undisclosed location overseas. Without taking any questions from journalists, the iconoclastic Flynn removed his bowler hat, humbly bowed his head to the flashing cameras, and quietly left the building never to be seen or heard of again.

♦ ♦ ♦

And so it was that Mortimer Flynn, aged forty-three and at the height of his power, exited the world stage. We now know from his diaries that following the infamous press conference, Flynn and his family sailed to Wales under aliases and the cover of disguise, where they lived in complete isolation for almost two years in the humblest of rural cottages, waiting for the newspapers to tire of their story. On the whole this was a peaceful time for the family, free from the burdens of public life and the pressures of big business, but there always remained a deep uncertainty about what the future held in store.

During this time Mortimer remained extremely withdrawn, spending the best part of every day and night in his study, immersing himself in the great works of philosophy and religion, both Eastern and Western. When he was not studying, he would meditate, leaving the family to go about their days almost as if he were not there. Although he spoke occasionally of his inner struggles and the causes of his anxiety, he was unable to express himself beyond a certain point, and his wife, Elizabeth, did not force the issue. She could see that Mortimer did not yet have any answers.

♦ ♦ ♦

One day, as the children were outside playing in the fields under the morning sun, Mortimer invited Elizabeth into his study where, at long last, something of an explanation was attempted. He began, as he knew he must, with an apology, expressing his great sorrow for all the uncertainty he had caused her and the children, and most of all for not being able to talk in much detail about the reasons for his actions until now. The only point he offered in mitigation was that until now his reasons had been too unclear, although he did not use this as a basis to seek forgiveness. He also acknowledged with the deepest gratitude the love and tolerance she had shown him, which, after all he had done, he knew he did not deserve.

After saying this much, Mortimer hung his head, and a long, deafening silence followed, softened only by the faint sound of children laughing in the distance. Perfectly still, Elizabeth sat before him with deceptive calmness, showing no signs that her entire universe was spinning to the point of nausea. She began to agonise when she realised that her husband was not searching for words but rather trying to build up the courage to speak the words he had already found.

Eventually, as a single tear rolled down his cheek, Mortimer raised his grey eyes to look at his wife, and once again he began to speak. Having quietened whatever demons had been taunting his spirit, his words now flowed easily, as if liquidated by the unqualified honesty that was driving them out. He spoke at length of how intensely disillusioned he had become with his material success in the world, the emptiness of its pleasures, and the shallowness of its glamour. None of his achievements, he maintained, had ever satisfied his craving for meaning; they merely served as a comfortable distraction that kept him busy as he frittered away his life. In a similar vein he spoke of the confusion of his desires, of how he had been chasing dreams that were not his own, and of how achieving those dreams had come to haunt his soul in ways that, ultimately, he could no longer endure. Less abstractly, he confessed to never liking the people that he invited to his parties – not one of them – and yet he admitted with as much shame as disappointment that all his efforts had been subconsciously motivated by the desire to have these people like him and envy him, as if they were the judges of his worth and therefore the people he must impress. But in dedicating his life to seeking the favour and respect of these upper-class fools, he had come to see that there was no greater fool than he.

Mortimer offered all this as an explanation for his breakdown, which he insisted was not a psychological breakdown but a spiritual one. As he said, it was not his mind that had become sick, but his soul. This was the vague, unclassifiable spiritual condition that had kept him bed-ridden for all those months, and which ultimately led to the rejection of his corporate empire. He suggested it was not so much a break*down*, then, as it was a break*through*. Having slowly awakened to the inauthenticity of his life's story, he had realised that he could not in good conscience continue playing the character he had written for himself. It therefore became necessary for him to shed his identity, as a snake sheds its skin, and create someone new. But who he was to become, he explained to his wife, was an internal riddle he had not yet solved.

♦ ♦ ♦

Elizabeth listened to all this uneasily but also with strange relief, as if she had somehow always known that these words needed to be spoken. Deep down, perhaps, she had always wanted to speak similar words herself, *to herself*, but had not yet found the courage. She might not have understood her husband's struggles, or her own, with much clarity, but she had known of them in the depths of her being, at the level of unprocessed sensibility. In other words, she was somehow aware that she and her husband had been living a fake, fragile life, one moulded strictly by the world's influences, pressures, and expectations, and thus, despite appearances, not a life of their own shaping at all. What she had never expected, however – could never have expected – were the words that would come next from Mortimer's mouth. She had assumed that her husband's confession, so to speak – the baring of his soul – was essentially over; that he had already said everything of consequence. But she was mistaken.

♦ ♦ ♦

Mortimer shifted in his chair and seemed to tense up, the life in his eyes appearing to implode into nothingness. His words no longer flowed so smoothly and for a time they dried up completely, once again engendering a deep anxiety in his wife, who remained as still as stone. But after another painfully long silence, Mortimer was able to finish what he had to say. He knew that there was no easy way to finish his confession, so he just took a deep breath, looked blankly downward at some indistinct object on the floor of his study, and said what he had to say in the clearest terms possible. He did not bother with pleasantries or euphemisms, for he knew that in the circumstances these would have been very out of place, and given that he did not need to censor his language with etiquette or stylistic conventions, this made it easier for the words to find their way out.

In a quiet voice Mortimer explained that for the past year or so – ever since his breakdown – he had been trying to decide whether or not to kill himself. This revelation set off yet another long silence, which was broken only by Elizabeth who quietly repeated the statement back to him, as if checking she had heard correctly, to which Mortimer responded by quietly repeating his difficult words once more: yes, he had been trying to decide whether or not to kill himself. If this blunt admission were not distressing enough, Mortimer then added that after all his recent readings and meditations on the human condition, the most he could say to the question of whether life was worth living was that he was not yet sure. Is it not so, he asked rhetorically, that suffering and horror lie at the core of existence? Were not violence, misery, and injustice rife in every corner of the world? Was not nature red in tooth and claw? If so, he whispered to himself, could existence ever be justified?

Mortimer looked up and assured his wife, who had gone a deathly pale, that given his uncertainty over life's justification, he was not about to kill himself – at least, not yet. But he did not and, indeed, could not assure her that the question of suicide was off the table. In fact, he felt obliged to make it very clear that the question was still very open. In some sense he felt it was the most important question he could ever ask himself – the most important question humans could ever ask themselves – and yet he lamented the fact that none of his teachers, in any of the prestigious colleges at which he was educated, had ever dared to raise it. Was this because they too were unsure about whether life could be answered in the affirmative? He suspected that this was so.

Having managed to raise the question of suicide for himself, however, and having passionately explored its depths in the darkness and solitude of his bedroom back in Texas, Mortimer explained that he had turned to the great texts of philosophy and religion in search of answers, as soon as he had the freedom and opportunity to do so. This was why he had locked himself up in his study for the past two years, reading voraciously and meditating on the many potent insights he discovered waiting for him in books. But although the time he spent in internal dialogue with the great philosophers, prophets, and theologians had been necessary and of the greatest assistance, he had come to realise that whatever it was that he was seeking, this must be found, if it even exists, not in books, but in the world of *lived experience*. Upon these grounds Mortimer explained that in order to continue exploring the question of whether human existence was justifiable, he felt he needed to give up his abstract wanderings in metaphysics and religion, and instead place his faith in the concrete domain of scientific inquiry. Dissatisfied with his armchair perspective, he declared that he could no longer merely ponder life; he felt compelled to experiment with life instead, to test certain hypotheses that he had formulated about the human situation.

At this stage the anxiety that had been consuming Elizabeth transformed into a burning intrigue. She had heard of scientists testing hypotheses about everything from the number of electrons in an atom to the distance between galaxies, but she had never heard of scientists testing the question of whether *life itself* was justifiable. Furthermore, she had not the faintest idea of how, or even whether, this could be done. What on earth was her husband talking about?

Had he at last gone mad?

♦ ♦ ♦

Mortimer abruptly stood up and began pacing slowly around the room, stating that if Elizabeth would indulge him for a short while longer, everything would be explained. His words now flowed freely, as if the floodgates had finally opened, and his wife saw that there was a fire burning in his eyes.

Put simply, what he wanted to know – that is to say, what he wanted to *test* – was whether human beings, under ideal, or near ideal conditions, could live free and flourishing lives in harmony with each other and with nature, without human relations tending towards domination and destruction. This, Mortimer maintained, was a true test of whether life should be affirmed, for he felt that if there were the real possibility of a just and prosperous society of humans arising in the future, this would provide some justification today for humankind continuing the seemingly futile and excruciating struggle for existence. If, however, human beings could not live in peace and prosperity, even under idealised conditions, then arguably humankind's struggle for existence was without justification. Indeed, Mortimer dispassionately noted that if his honest inquiry into the human condition were to demonstrate that life, at its core, was nothing but a tragic curse, and that love and joy were unable to balance the world's unfathomable suffering, he would probably consider his own suicide to be logically inescapable – according to his own logic, at least.

But he felt that he was getting ahead of himself here, talking of such gloomy results before he had even discussed his methodology. In order to test the question of whether the struggle for existence was justified, Mortimer explained that he had devised an ambitious experiment in living, which he hoped to begin undertaking as soon as possible. His plan was to use his vast financial resources to purchase an island somewhere – somewhere very isolated, in the hope of being left alone – and on this island establish an intentional community, through which he could test his existential hypotheses. Although he had not yet worked out all the details of this plan, the outline was clear enough: he would find and purchase a suitable island; fund the construction of whatever infrastructure was needed to support a human community; and then initiate an interview process through which he would select a certain number of people – perhaps fifteen hundred or two thousand – to live on the island and participate in his living experiment.

It was absolutely essential, he continued, that this intentional community be based on economically and environmentally sound principles, because if the results of this proposed experiment could not be replicated around the world and endlessly into the future, it seemed to him that it would shed very little light on the human situation. In other words, he had no interest in creating some temporary, artificial utopia that was dependent on his wealth or which could not be sustained over the long term due to its impact on nature. Rather, he wanted to create, or see if he could create, the foundations for a self-sufficient and environmentally sound community in which human beings were able to live freely, peacefully, and happily, under some system of self-government. This intentional community would be called

'Entropia', Mortimer announced, a term that alluded to the biophysical laws of nature upon which his utopian living experiment would be based.

There was one final point about this experiment that Mortimer wished to emphasise as being of the utmost importance. In all his readings of philosophy, religion, politics, history, and economics, Mortimer explained that there was one feature of the human condition that continued to arise again and again, across all cultures and times, albeit in different forms, and which he insisted was the primary cause of human suffering. The feature to which he referred was the failure of humankind to understand what he called the Principle of Sufficiency. Throughout history, he maintained, most human suffering was caused either by people not having sufficient material resources to live with dignity, or, by people having an insatiable greed for superfluous material wealth, and thereby never finding contentment in life no matter how wealthy they might become. It would seem to follow, Mortimer argued, that in order to avoid these two great causes of suffering, it was necessary for human beings to find and embrace 'the Middle Way' between having too little and wanting too much. Mortimer offered this as a simple way of framing the Principle of Sufficiency. During his studies he had been struck by the fact that this principle was found, in various forms, not only in all the major religious and spiritual texts of the world, but also in political writings across the political spectrum. It seemed, in fact, that the importance of material sufficiency to a well-lived life was one point, perhaps the only point, on which all the wisdom traditions of humankind had found unanimous agreement. Surely there was something to it! Indeed, Mortimer hypothesised that it provided the secret to human flourishing. He declared with exhilaration that his living experiment would test this hypothesis, by attempting to create a self-sufficient society based on lifestyles of material sufficiency – a society where everyone had enough, and, just as importantly, where everyone knew how much was enough. Could it be done? Could such a society prosper?

That remained to be seen.

♦ ♦ ♦

Mortimer brought his long oration to a close by stating that it was his intention to live on the island himself as an ordinary member of the community, without disclosing his identity, in order to experience and observe the results of his experiment first hand. He hastened to add that it was his deepest desire that Elizabeth and the children would join him on this journey. After an indeterminate amount of time living in such a community – perhaps a decade or so – Mortimer felt that he would have a reasonably clear insight into whether the human situation could be justified, which he reiterated was the question burning in his eyes.

After slowly moving his way across his study, deep in thought, Mortimer paused by the window and looked across the fields to where his children were playing happily on the edge of the woods. It was a heavenly picture of peace and innocence, and for a moment, as the morning light shone on his face, Mortimer seemed perfectly calm.

♦ ♦ ♦

Over the next few days Mortimer and his wife were in constant dialogue about all that had been said, filling in the gaps and fleshing out the details. Although Elizabeth respectfully admitted that she found all the talk about suicide unnecessary and a bit misguided, she was quite aware that her husband had plunged deep into some perennial human questions and that his internal struggles were very real. She did sense, however, that Mortimer's struggles had subsided somewhat, as if merely speaking his words had somehow relieved him of a heavy burden. There was a new lightness to him, one that his wife had not seen in him before, and this brought them closer together. For the time being he stopped reading entirely, and he meditated only for a short time each morning. The rest of the day he would spend outside tending to the autumn garden with his wife, reconnecting with his children, and wandering in the surrounding woods like a lost poet, entranced by the simple delights of nature. Something had changed in Mortimer, as if he had drawn a line under some of his troubles, somehow containing and controlling them, even if he had not yet solved them.

On the issue of 'Entropia', Elizabeth needed no convincing. The world certainly needed a new direction, she said – Western cultures, in particular – and she was the first to agree that nothing would inspire change more than a real-world example of a better way. Accordingly, she considered the idea of creating a small island community that would seek to live within nature's limits to be a fascinating and potentially important social experiment, one that would receive her unconditional support. Not only did she feel it was an imaginative exploration of alternative ways of living and being, but she knew it would be a far nobler use of their vast financial resources than throwing extravagant soirees for the world's rich and famous, which she too had tired of long ago. Furthermore, she considered the project to be an exciting path away from their little hideaway cottage in the country, the solitude of which she said was beginning to weigh on her.

The job before them, then, was to turn the bold vision of Entropia into a concrete reality, a task that they both took to with dedication and zeal. Their lives were suddenly aglow with meaning and direction, and time began moving to a new rhythm.

♦ ♦ ♦

After weeks of searching, with the help of various agents, Mortimer and Elizabeth discovered an island in the middle of the South Pacific Ocean that met their broad requirements. Without too much difficulty they managed to purchase the island from the New Zealand government, in whose jurisdiction it fell, while also keeping their identities hidden, which remained their desire. The island had been kept as a nature reserve, and so it was uninhabited, but given its isolation and relatively small size, the government had decided, in the midst of an economic depression, that ultimately it was an unjustified expense. When an offer that could not be refused was tendered for its purchase, the struggling conservative government did not let the opportunity pass it by, eagerly selling this neglected national treasure to the anonymous bidder.

Spanning some eleven-and-a-half thousand hectares, the roughly crescent-shaped island boasted a lush landscape of rainforests, meadows, and rolling hills, with an abundance of arable land that was carved up in places by rivers and streams flowing from the small mount that lay on the island's eastern tip. On the northern edge, swamps and wetlands merged gradually with the ocean, expanding and contracting with the tides. Golden-brown sands, coral reefs, and turquoise waters circled the perimeter of the island, and within those borders nature was alive with all kinds of exotic plant and animal life. It was truly a place of natural splendour. When Mortimer and Elizabeth first set eyes on the Isle, they knew that if they could not create paradise here, they could do so nowhere. Its beauty was enough to induce a shudder of awe between the shoulder blades.

Once they had signed off on the purchase, they spent the best part of the next year designing, with the guidance of various expert advisors, the infrastructure needed for their intentional community to function: the houses, the buildings, the energy and utility services, and so forth. As soon as these plans were drawn up, construction and development began, and while that was taking place Mortimer and his wife began the process of finding willing participants to join them in this living experiment. In order to facilitate this process they decided to establish a transdisciplinary university on the Isle, which they were to call the Academy of Walden, and this allowed them to invite a broad range of students and teachers to apply for an indeterminate residency. Before long the applications started flowing in.

It was made very clear from the outset that successful applicants would be establishing an experimental community, and that university life would be but one aspect of a broader social experience, which would include working in the local economy to help provide for the community's needs. Prospective students and teachers were advised further that they would be welcome (with their immediate families) to live on the island for as long as they wanted – their whole lives, if they wished – but that if they ever chose to leave, they could never return. This, it was explained, was purely an attempt to encourage members to stay for as long as possible, in order to promote a stable community. By the time the Isle was ready to be inhabited there were approximately seventeen hundred selected individuals from every ethnic, cultural, academic, and artistic background imaginable, all ready and willing to take up residency in Entropia at a moment's notice.

And thus the experiment began!

♦ ♦ ♦

Unsurprisingly, the first few months on the island were a festival of chaos and excitement. All manner of systems needed to be established in order to get the community functioning, so formal classes in the Academy were delayed for some time. But eventually, after overcoming administrative problems of various sorts, life on the Isle fell into a certain rhythm. Evening lectures started being organised; the farms on the periphery of the residential blocks started producing food; and a flourishing and inclusive social life developed. Everyone seemed to be aware that they were a part of something extraordinary, something truly unique in the history of humankind, and this realisation gave rise to a spirit of goodwill that seemed capable of solving any problems that arose. If nothing else, this first phase in the experiment was an impressive display of leaderless self-organisation.

During these early months Mortimer managed to integrate himself into the experiment well enough, as an ordinary member of the community. He taught introductory classes on mechanics and algebra, and attended various classes on subjects ranging from art history to horticulture. He even started taking cello lessons, which secretly had been a lifelong dream of his, and he proved to have a natural flair for the instrument. Having grown a long beard during his time in the cottage, as well as having lost a considerable amount of weight, nobody ever recognised this amateur cellist as the imposing oil magnate he once was: he now went by the name Janus Bifrons, after the two-faced god of beginnings and transitions. Elizabeth's identity remained similarly undisclosed, assisted by various simple changes to her hair and style of dress. She immediately flourished on the Isle, having been freed from the materialistic and patriarchal culture that for too long had stifled her innate vitality. It was as if their old life had been drawn in the sand but was now washed away by a new tide, never to reappear.

Over the next few years Mortimer was heartened by the progress made in the community, and it can be inferred from his good spirits that he had put the question of suicide to rest, encouraged by his wife's counsel, no doubt. The Academy was proving to be a great success, evidenced by the fact that the libraries and gardens on the Isle were always full of people exploring and developing their latest intellectual passions. Furthermore, various guilds spontaneously arose, providing expert training in a vast array of practical skills, such as building, sewing, and gardening. Other guilds offered instruction in the fine arts – anything from painting to sculpture to music, as well as everything in between and beyond. Every night there would be live concerts in one of the various halls, or under the stars in the central garden, where musicians, poets, and storytellers would come together and perform their latest compositions, or experiment with new aesthetic styles and combinations. As well as a thriving cultural and social life, the productive foundations of the community had developed considerably, with especially well organised systems of food production and distribution. On the whole, people seemed to be living simply, happily, and cooperatively, and this gave Mortimer a sense that his experiment was meeting with some success.

Nevertheless, it became clear to Mortimer quite early on that his hopes for economic self-sufficiency had been extremely ambitious, and in fact that his expectations in this regard had been quite naive. Although the farms were well developed and provided a significant portion of the community's food, much food was still imported. All manner of other things also needed to be imported, such as tools, medicines, paper, fabric, glass, and machinery, because the systems needed to produce these things, in the amount required, had not yet been established. A large amount of oil and coal was also imported, and the consumption of these energy sources even seemed to be increasing. Obviously Mortimer was perfectly capable of funding all the necessary imports, which he did, and he had even set up a trust fund to continue funding necessary expenses well into the future. But he recognised, with some unease, that this meant that there was an underlying artificiality to life on the Isle, given how much of the community's requirements still depended on the imports he funded. Would the community eventually wean itself off the imports and his financial support? Could life as they knew it be sustained if they relied only on the resources provided for them on the island?

These were questions that Mortimer ultimately took to his grave.

♦ ♦ ♦

It would be of some historical and sociological interest, no doubt, to describe in detail the form of life that developed on the Isle during these early decades of the Entropia experiment. After all, the circumstances were extraordinary, to say the least, and readers might well have questions about what life was like on the Isle. However, the fact that the experiment remained dependent on Mortimer's financial support means that Entropia, at least in this early period, can shed very little light on the questions of human existence that had originally motivated Mortimer to create the experiment. In other words, Entropia may well have been as close as humankind ever got to a real-world utopia, but given its financial dependency, it was ultimately little more than an expensive and enjoyable social experiment, one that could never be universalised or self-sustaining, at least in its original form.

But the nature of Entropia changed forever when, a little over seven decades ago, the Great Disruption marked the collapse of industrial civilisation and the global economy upon which it was based. Almost overnight this catastrophic series of events completely cut the Isle off from the supply of imports it had been relying on, leaving the community to fend for itself as best it could. Everyone on the Isle suddenly discovered that they were no longer part of a comfortable living experiment with artificial economic foundations, but were instead facing the very real challenges of sustaining life after the crash. Admittedly, this community was better placed to deal with these harsh circumstances than perhaps any other on the planet, but that did not mean things were easy. Far from it! This was a prolonged period of significant hardship, in which the fabric of their society was tested to the extreme. Nevertheless, it was also an uplifting period that exemplified the human spirit at its noblest, and the society that was produced is of much greater and more lasting significance to the human story than its antecedent form, prior to the crash. It is this second phase in the history of Entropia that will be the subject of this book, and for reasons that will be explained, this story is perhaps more relevant today than ever before.

It is hoped that this story might serve as something of a lantern in the dark and troubled times that lie ahead.

In closing this introduction, allow me to take a more personal stance. I have had the privilege of spending the first thirty-three years of my life on the Isle, as a member of the third generation since the Great Disruption. This leaves me well placed to describe, from an insider's perspective, at least, the nature of Entropia's post-crash era. I am also a part-time lecturer in philosophy and culture at the Academy, as well as an assistant editor of one of our local newspapers, so it is my job to stay informed about the most important current events on the Isle. Additionally, my studies have left me with an intimate understanding of the most significant events in our community's history. Presumably it was for these reasons that my peers invited me to write this book, an invitation I accepted with the utmost humility, knowing that the fullness of life on the Isle could never be captured in words – not even in a shelf of books, let alone in this single volume. In this sense, my very attempt to describe Entropia's economy, culture, and politics is evidence enough that I have failed in my task. I am aware, furthermore, that the following account of Entropia will be shaped inevitably by my personal experiences on the Isle, so I cannot make any claims to the objectivity of my account. However, I have been assisted greatly in writing this book by the goodwill of my peers, who have entrusted to me their many journals and diaries, which I have studied closely and drawn upon where appropriate in an attempt to expand the limits of my own perspective and broaden my understanding. For that trust, I am immensely grateful.

♦ ♦ ♦

By the time the Great Disruption hit, the lineage of Mortimer and Elizabeth Flynn had already come to an end, because neither of their two children had children of their own. Nevertheless, the questions that originally inspired Entropia live on, and I offer this book as commentary on the lessons we have learned on the journey so far. Whether readers find this offering worthwhile, I cannot know in advance, but I can say that putting the story of Entropia into words has crystallised much about our way of life that I had previously understood only at the level of raw experience. As an old philosopher once said, life must be lived forwards, but it can only be understood backwards.

2

THE DISINTEGRATION OF EMPIRE

The picture of Entropia that I will endeavour to paint in this book does not begin with a blank canvas. Our community was, and is, a creature of its time, and our way of life on the Isle can only be understood in relation to the collapse of industrial civilisation out of which it emerged. Accordingly, I feel the nature of that collapse must be described, or at least outlined, in order to make clear why our society took the form it did.

Before sketching that history of collapse, however, it is worth acknowledging that no matter how well our economy and broader society may be functioning today, we have not been able to escape – nor did we ever think we could escape – those darker, painful elements in life that are built into the human condition. I feel this is an important acknowledgement to make, because I do not wish to give the impression, or give rise to the expectation, that our way of life on the Isle is or has been free from difficulty, grief, and strife. I assure you, Entropia is no utopia! We are human! And that means we are as susceptible to suffering as any other community. I will not dwell on these grim themes for long, but to give some tonal balance to the picture this book will paint, some darker shades must be introduced from the outset, at least around these foundational edges.

Let me begin by stating the obvious: the Great Disruption was by far and away the most destabilising and traumatic series of events our community has ever had to endure. While I was not alive during this tumultuous period, and so cannot speak from experience, it is an historical era that is given prolonged attention in our schools and the Academy, so all of us are very familiar with it, even though we now only have the distanced perspective of historical scholarship. My understanding of this period is also enriched by the many stories my grandparents used to tell me when they were still alive. My grandmother, in particular, was an engaging storyteller, and her soft-spoken but vivid anecdotes about the Great Disruption taught me that human suffering is always personal, always specific, no matter how broadly it is shared. It hurt *here*, she would explain, and it felt like *this*. She would speak not so much of hunger in the abstract, as of the time the bean crop failed; not of loss, but of her own shattered dreams of security; not of pain, but of grandfather's arthritis, which he endured silently as he worked in the vineyards and orchards in the hope of feeding the community he loved. She would speak of how the sparkle in a friend's eyes forever disappeared as a result of spiralling despair, and of the quiet sadness she could see in the eyes of every parent who could not assure their children that the future would be kind and safe. Most striking of all was my grandmother's account of the Isle's only suicide – the melancholy story of a young Tibetan woman called Nishka, for whom the Great Disruption was too much to bear. A genuine prodigy of the violin, and blessed with a face of penetrating beauty, Nishka seemingly could not find solace even in our warm community, choosing instead to take her own life in a warm bath – violin in hand. On the wooden stool next to the bath she left a composition, entitled 'Avoiding the Rush', to which even today only the brave-hearted dare to listen. The melody too easily evokes the harrowing image of a girl playing her own requiem in a bath, with bloodied wrists. Naturally, such events shook the community to the core, but the gut-wrenching images and emotions they evoke help to humanise an era that otherwise might be too easily intellectualised by those of us who came later.

The first issue to highlight, then, is that the Great Disruption brought with it widespread anxiety, fear, and often tremendous suffering – like any radical discontinuity in social and economic life would be expected to do. Although we had been transitioning for many years toward self-sufficiency, our way of life at the time remained highly dependent on imports of industrially produced food and materials. What is more, despite the fact that 'building resilience' was high on our list of stated priorities, when the cargo ships suddenly stopped arriving, the social and economic shocks we faced were by no means painlessly absorbed. We may have been better placed than most of humankind, but as the Great Disruption shook the world and isolated us permanently from the rest of civilisation, we found ourselves grossly underprepared, both mentally and in terms of our social and economic systems. In retrospect we see that many of our attempts to build resilience were really little more than pleasant, well-intentioned games, which did little to absorb the shocks that were eventually delivered upon us. At the same time, perhaps some things just cannot be prepared for, however diligently a community might try.

In the face of civilisational collapse, the internal or psychological shocks typically hit first. Human beings are creatures of habit and custom, and we have an overwhelming tendency to assume tomorrow will be similar to today. Even when we see our world falling down around us, calling for an urgent and sustained response, we divert our gaze in an attempt to distance ourselves from the radical changes that are announcing themselves on the horizon. But wilful blindness in the face of civilisational deterioration is at best a short-sighted strategy, one that ultimately leads to the crash just hitting harder and louder, and with the distressing element of surprise. It is like watching a balloon being blown up, breath by breath, and assuming that since no breath so far has burst the balloon, adding more air should not produce any great changes. And so we go about our days, business as usual. When we wake to our new circumstances, however – as the balloon bursts violently – we find that the world we knew has been shattered, and our insides begin to twist with the angst of terrifying uncertainty. We complain that nobody warned us; that we could not possibly have known. But we were warned, we did know, and now our inaction looks not just foolish but shameful.

Coming to terms, psychologically, with the Great Disruption was challenging enough. It was as if our parent civilisation had committed suicide, tragically leaving our community orphaned and alone. Cut off from the Old World, our universe suddenly seemed a whole lot smaller and our minds had to adjust to this new cosmology. But soon the sheer physical reality hit home, which is to say, the fear of being hungry gave way to the physical experience of hunger itself. A collapsing civilisation does not wait for people to adjust mentally to the new circumstances. While everything was breaking down in chaos, testing people to the limits of their mental fortitude, it was precisely then when the physical dimensions of collapse became dominant, compounding our challenges. By this stage there was no time to sit around adjusting mentally to the new situation. Instead, urgent, practical questions had to be faced about how to secure the provision of basic material needs, especially food. Suddenly everyone was a farmer, a scavenger, a jack-of-all-trades, and an inventor.

Fortunately, as noted earlier, we had quite well-developed systems of local food production on the Isle, so nobody faced starvation, as such. Nevertheless, for some time, while we desperately expanded those systems after the crash, our diets were significantly tightened. Instead of three meals a day, we had one or two. The variety of food was also limited to the most productive and nutritious crops, such as beans, potatoes, and lentils, although people did not lament the lack of variety, for they were grateful simply to have enough food to survive. Most people began to look worryingly thin, and they carried the mental and physical strain of the circumstances in their eyes.

Innumerable things our community once took for granted – conveniences and comforts that we once considered necessities – were no longer available. Everything, it seemed, was scarce: from food, to medicine, to materials. Soon enough our material standard of living barely resembled what preceded it, in ways that will be discussed further in due course. We endured these material privations stoically, however, determined to struggle onwards through this period of trial with our community and spirit of positivity more or less intact. There were social conflicts too, of course – such as the long, heated debates over how much of our minimal oil and coal reserves to use, and for what purposes – but generally these were measured, mature conflicts. Everyone knew that there was no place for childish egoism in times of social distress and economic crisis.

My point in briefly reviewing this period is simply to highlight the fact that our community, far from having a smooth or idyllic commencement, was born of struggle and considerable hardship. Nevertheless, even the clouds of a violent thunderstorm can have a silver lining. As it happened, this early, post-crash period shaped us in ways that are still with us, for what did not kill us made us stronger.

There is obviously much more to say about how our community dealt with its isolation, and this book will describe our existing way of life in detail, as it has taken form roughly seven decades after the crash. This chapter, however, presents an historical review of industrial civilisation's rise and demise, because this is necessary to provide a backdrop against which life on the Isle today can be fully understood. At first this may seem like rather too dark and heavy a foundation, but the flourishing sufficiency economy we have created on the Isle will seem clearest when defined in contrast to the industrialised, growth economies of the Old World, which now lie in ruins.

Fortunately, I have in my possession an old essay, dated 8 June 2031, written a few years after the Great Disruption, which provides a remarkably concise, if somewhat polemical, history of this collapse. I shall reproduce this essay below, knowing that I am unable to improve it. At some stage over the course of recent generations the author's name was lost, or perhaps the essay was originally published anonymously – a practice that was not altogether uncommon on the Isle in earlier generations. Whatever the case, that issue need not concern us presently. What is important is that our journey through Entropia is given some historical context, and the following essay serves that purpose well. As the great poet, Thomas Hardy, once wrote: 'If a path to the better there be, it begins with a full look at the worst'.

On that basis, I present the essay:

♦ ♦ ♦

Reflections on the Great Disruption

Those who cannot remember the past are condemned to repeat it.
– George Santayana

Karl Marx, capitalism's preeminent critic, believed that he had uncovered the laws of history, on the basis of which he predicted that there would inevitably come a time when capitalism would come to an end. He believed that human beings would never stop fighting for justice – no matter how hopeless things got – and this gave him confidence that the injustices he considered inherent to capitalism would one day be overturned. Just as the slaves had overthrown their lords, and just as the bourgeoisie had overthrown the aristocracy, Marx concluded that it was inevitable that eventually the working classes of the world would overthrow the capitalist class. This was the revolution, or series of revolutions, that would usher in a communist utopia, representing the true end of history. It was not a question of 'if', but only 'when'. Of course, owing to the fact that the rich and powerful would never voluntarily give up their unjustifiable privileges, it followed that the communist revolutions would almost certainly have to be violent revolutions. From a Marxist perspective, at least, it seemed that there was no other way for a post-capitalist society to emerge.

However, as early capitalism developed into the global economic system it became in the late 20th century – a system that we now know as Empire – the prospects of a global communist revolution seemed less and less likely, even as the moral and ecological critiques of capitalism seemed ever more relevant and penetrating. While there was certainly deep and widespread discontent among the world's people – even if they did not always understand the fundamental causes of their discontent – Empire had a way of distracting people and indeed entire nations from developing any latent revolutionary ambitions. This was done primarily through the lure of consumer goods and the promise of globalising the 'American Dream', a technique of seduction that proved remarkably successful at quashing oppositional sentiments before they even reached the level of consciousness. Many people found themselves locked into a consumer existence, unable to imagine any alternative; many more others, of course, were locked into extreme poverty by the same system, left to imagine alternatives they were unable to realise. If, on very rare occasions, the working classes did manage to organise themselves with subversive intent, the capitalist state always showed itself to be willing and able to suppress or fragment all uprisings that threatened the status quo. Thus Empire marched on, extending its reach to all corners of the globe, brutally shaping the world according to its cold logic of profit-maximisation. Money, not man, became the measure of all things. Man had lost control.

Nevertheless, those in the orthodox Marxist tradition still clung to the hope that their progressive conception of history would prove to be correct. The working classes, they maintained, would eventually become aware both that they were being robbed by the capitalist system and that collectively they had the power to stop such robbery. It was predicted that through the development and expansion of this 'class consciousness', capitalism would finally fall by way of revolution. Again, it was believed that this scenario was built into the laws of history, just as gravity is built into the laws of physics. There was to be no escaping it.

Little did Marx and his left-wing disciples know, however, that capitalism would indeed fall, but not by way of *revolution* – by way of *collapse*. This was a potential outcome to which the tradition gave almost no attention, primarily because capitalism transformed over the course of the 20th century in ways that Marx could not possibly have predicted from his 19th century perspective. Scathingly critical of almost every aspect of capitalism, Marx was nevertheless admiring of its productive capacity, but what he never put his mind to was the possibility that capitalism's great productive capacity, which was supposedly its greatest asset, would actually become the driving force behind its own demise. More precisely, Marx never foresaw that capitalism, far from being overthrown by a proletarian revolution, would actually grow itself to death, like a cancer cell, leaving in its wake not a communist utopia, but the many faces of deindustrial civilisation. This inevitable outcome of growth is a form of purgatory, one might say, from which humanity has yet to emerge, and indeed may never emerge. For what it is worth, the growth economies of communism would have led humankind down the very same path, had they been globalised.

As life 'beyond civilisation' begins – not with a bang but a whimper – there may be some value in looking back on the disintegration of Empire, if only so that we may better understand the present as we look to the future. Accordingly, let us reflect on the basic dynamics of this period of collapse, and examine its underlying historical causes, in the hope that humankind might avoid ever condemning itself to repeat this tragic story.

Energy as the Lifeblood of Civilisation

If there is one factor that defines the rise and fall of civilisations more than any other, it is energy. Energy is the physical basis for development, the lifeblood of civilisation. It is the tool we use to try to solve our problems, even if its use can also cause those problems. Historically, when an affordable supply of energy could meet energy demand, civilisations grew in size, strength, and complexity. Problems were solved and things would seem to progress. When civilisations expanded beyond their sustainable capacity, however, and energy surpluses dried up, new problems or existential threats would arise that could not be solved – wars, ecosystemic change, disease, etc. – and solutions to existing problems could not always be maintained. Consequently, progress would come to an end and begin to turn back on itself.

In such times national debt would be vastly increased, or currencies would be debased, in an attempt to fabricate energy and at least maintain the status quo. But borrowing from the future in this way was simply the precursor to economic collapse. Money is not energy. Wars would also arise as competing political forces saw opportunities to advance, but military expenditure would simply draw more energy and funds away from maintaining social systems and infrastructure, generally leading to the fragmentation or breakdown of centralised systems of administration, governance, and rule.

No matter how robust and glorious a civilisation might once have seemed, all of them throughout history have eventually entered the downward spiral of deterioration and collapse. There seems to be no escaping this tragic reoccurrence. It seems to be built into the fabric of human society, although every civilisation claims to be different – until it collapses. Collapse means involuntary simplification and economic contraction, whereby individuals and communities are forced to give up their old, energy-intensive ways of living and adopt a radically lower material standard of living. Tragically but inevitably, collapse also means significant population die-off, as the energy required to maintain sufficient food production and distribution becomes unavailable, resulting in widespread famine, disease, and death. Entrenched power structures are also destabilised in such times, inviting social disorder and opening up space for new power struggles to emerge in the forms of civil and international conflict. So it was throughout history, and as outlined below, these essential dynamics also coloured the rise and fall of humankind's first truly global civilisation – Empire.

Seeds of Empire

Let us begin this autopsy way back on the edge of prehistory. The transition from hunter-gatherer societies to agricultural societies was not so much a revolution in food production as it was a revolution in energy supply. It is in this transition that the seeds of Empire were sown. The nature of hunter-gatherer societies was dictated by the limitations of energy supply, for there was no energy surplus to maintain much social complexity. The modest energy available primarily came in the forms of food and fire, and these modest supplies meant that complex social, economic or political institutions could not be supported. Through the uptake of agriculture, however, which was vastly more productive than hunting and gathering, humankind was able to secure increased energy supply through its increased food supply. This meant that fewer people were required to dedicate their time and energies to food production, because they could be supported by a sub-section of the population – farmers.

Civilisations accordingly began to develop increasing numbers of 'non-food' specialists – people who were freed from the task of sourcing or producing food and who therefore could dedicate their time to such things such as building houses, producing more tools and weapons, forming an army, or taking on leadership or bureaucratic roles of governance, education, and administration. In this way agricultural societies began to develop increasing levels of social complexity, which required an increasing supply of energy to maintain. The increased energy supply also provided the foundations for population growth, although at first that growth was modest.

It should be noted that hunter-gatherer societies did not always adopt agricultural practices such as planting seeds, or domesticating animals, as soon as they discovered them. In many cases, there was a period of hundreds or even thousands of years between discovering agriculture and adopting it (and the transition was often gradual rather than abrupt). This was because, from the perspective of hunter-gatherers, the transition did not immediately seem to be an obvious advance. With few material needs, hunter-gatherers found that they could provide for themselves with only two or three hours labour each day. An agricultural existence, however, despite being more productive, required working much harder, and without much to show for it (at least at first). Indeed, anthropologists have studied the fossils of early farming communities and discovered that their skeletons are typically shorter than those of hunter-gatherers, indicating a reduced nutritional intake. Furthermore, by being sedentary (as opposed to nomadic), agricultural societies faced new sanitary issues arising from the accumulation of human and animal excrement, and this gave rise to diseases that actually reduced the average lifespan of individuals in early agricultural societies, compared with hunter-gatherers. Without wanting to romanticise hunter-gatherer societies – which of course had their own limitations and problems – one can nevertheless understand why they were often doubtful about the merits of agriculture as a way of life.

All the same, no matter how much hunter-gatherers might have preferred their materially simple but leisure-rich existences, there were certain realities that came to influence their calculus. Most importantly, when neighbouring tribes or societies adopted agriculture, their numbers and power increased by virtue of their increased energy supplies, even if at first their standard of living also decreased in some respects. Their power increased, as noted above, because agriculture provided enough food for parts of the population to be employed solely as warriors or soldiers, and other parts of the population to make or develop more sophisticated weapons, armour, defences, etcetera. This created a power imbalance between agricultural and hunter-gatherer societies, and the latter were provided therefore with a strong incentive to adopt agriculture – not for the reason of increasing their standard of living, but merely to avoid being eradicated by their increasingly powerful farming neighbours. Humankind thus became entangled in a form of 'arms race', from which, as we know, it was never able to escape.

Was Agriculture a Mistake?

As well as locking humankind into an arms race, the other way in which agriculture sowed the seeds of Empire was how it required enforceable property rules. Nomadic peoples were free to wander a sparsely populated Earth, and they did not need property rules to protect their 'wealth' because they would only accumulate as much as they could safely carry. But when societies went to the effort of cultivating land and tending to crops, they obviously had an incentive to defend that land from intruders, in order to reap where they had sown. Furthermore, sedentary societies were much more inclined to accumulate wealth, houses, and land, because they did not have to carry their possessions or assets everywhere they went. (In an aside, housing also initiated the disconnection of humankind from nature, in ways that over time would become insidiously harmful). Monetary systems, which arose in agricultural societies, also made accumulation much easier.

All this led to social and economic inequality becoming much more pronounced, which contrasted with the egalitarian nature of hunter-gatherer societies. Where once the world was held in common, agriculture created the need to distinguish between 'mine' and 'thine', a distinction that Jean-Jacques Rousseau was correct to suggest is the true foundation of civilisation:

> *The first man who, having enclosed a piece of ground, bethought himself of saying 'This is mine', and found people simple enough to believe him, was*

the real founder of civil society. From how many crimes, wars, and murders, from how many horrors and misfortunes might not anyone have saved mankind, by pulling up the stakes, or filling in the ditch, and crying to his fellows: 'Beware of listening to this imposter; you are undone if you once forget that the fruits of the earth belong to us all, and the earth itself to nobody'.

At first tribes and societies created boundaries, fences, and walls around their farms and territories, into which 'others' were not entitled to tread. Not long after, personal relationships within agricultural societies became similarly structured by property claims and disputes. This established a way of thinking that eventually gave rise to laws and governments, which were created to protect property interests – the property interests of the rich and powerful, at least. By this stage, for better or for worse, most human beings were no longer tribal wanderers, but increasingly citizens or subjects of a kingdom or state.

Notably, agriculture also laid the foundations for slavery, an institution that was essentially unknown in hunter-gatherer societies, if only for pragmatic reasons. Leaving moral issues to one side, it was simply uneconomic for hunter-gatherers to maintain slavery, because the benefits of slavery did not outweigh the costs. That is, it was easier to hunt for one's own food than to try to force others to do it. In contrast, the sedentary nature of agricultural societies, and the emergence of non-food specialists which agriculture supported, changed this calculus, making slavery an 'economic' means for a society to gain further energy supply through enforced labour. This established a 'ruling class' and an 'under-class', laying further foundations for Empire.

Starting from around 10,000 years ago, therefore, humankind increasingly looked to agriculture as a way of life, primarily because it provided the most energy. This transition also introduced new diseases, slavery, property rights, governments, standing armies, inequality, and class relations. Was it worth it? Perhaps this was humankind's greatest mistake. Or perhaps it was a necessary experiment that just happened to be conducted disastrously. Whatever the case, adopting agriculture was like crossing the Rubicon: having once done so, a society could never return.

Fossil Fuels and the Growth Model of Progress

For thousands of years human civilisations rose and fell without there being any revolutionary changes to the types of energy that human beings employed. Food remained the primary energy source (for human labour, as well as animal labour), and wood was used to fuel fires for cooking, light, and warmth. As basic technologies developed, there was also limited use of hydro energy, through waterwheels, and wind energy, through boats and windmills. Early in the 18th century, however, humankind's relationship to energy changed fundamentally, primarily due to the invention of the steam engine. This invention allowed human beings for the first time to harness, on a large scale, the truly immense energies stored in the fossil fuels – coal, at first, and later natural gas and oil.

These technological and energy advances ignited an explosion of mechanised economic activity that we now refer to as the industrial revolution. Increasing numbers of people were forced or seduced away from their farms and into urban factories, and a vast rail network emerged which allowed commodities to be traded and transported around continents with relative ease. Three centuries of unprecedented economic growth followed, which produced an exponential rise in material standards of living, primarily in Western societies but eventually elsewhere. For the first time the prospect of globalising affluence through mechanised production entered the human imagination. Industrial civilisation had been born, founded upon fossil fuels.

Within those nations that progressed from circumstances of widespread poverty to circumstances of moderate or comfortable material security, the human lot seemed to improve considerably. Although there were always costs, sometimes great costs, associated with economic growth – such as factory labour, pollution, deforestation, and social dislocation – for many decades these costs were seemingly outweighed by the material benefits that resulted. This perceived success led to the entrenchment of what political and economic historians now refer to as 'the growth model of progress'.

Put simply, the growth model assumed that the overall wellbeing of a society was approximately proportional to the size of its economy, because more money or higher Gross Domestic Product (GDP) meant that more individual and social desires could be satisfied via market transactions. No matter how rich a society became, growing the economy was thought to be the only effective way to eliminate poverty, reduce inequality and unemployment, properly fund schools, hospitals, the arts, scientific research, environmental protection programs, and so on. In other words, the underlying social problem (even within the richest nations) was believed to be a lack of money. Economic growth therefore was heralded across the political spectrum as the goal towards which societies across the globe should be directing their collective energies. The notion of a macro-economic 'optimal scale' was all but unthinkable. It was assumed that a bigger economy was always better.

For three centuries, then, fossil fuels provided humankind with the cheap and abundant sources of energy needed to pursue economic growth without apparent limit. Those fossil fuels also provided the energy foundations for exponential growth in population, which was more a side effect of industrial civilisation than an intentional aim. When once the earth appeared relatively empty, over the course of the 20th century it became full-to-overflowing.

Uneconomic Growth, Commodity Fetishism, and the Technocratic Faith

The growth model of progress, as we now know, turned out to be severely flawed, although dislodging it from the social imagination proved exceedingly difficult. John Stuart Mill, writing in 1848, was one of the first to point out that the costs of economic growth may one day exceed the benefits, at which time, he argued, the most appropriate form of economic governance would be 'the stationary state'. By this he meant a condition of zero growth in population and physical capital stock, but with continued improvement in what he called 'the Art of Living'. This aspect of his oeuvre, however – today his most famous – was either ignored or summarily dismissed by his contemporaries, and for many generations it lay forgotten in the intellectual dustbin. Although small groups of theorists and activists would try to revive and popularise its wisdom, limitless growth remained the overriding objective of governments across the globe. Indeed, it became clear that the market imperatives of capitalism meant that Empire had to grow or die.

Early in the 21st century, as the social and environmental costs of economic growth became more pronounced and harder to tolerate or ignore, the undercurrent of growth scepticism strengthened. Many rigorous sociological studies showed that economic growth in affluent societies had stopped contributing significantly to human wellbeing; that is, it became clear that a rise in material 'standards of living' was no longer strongly correlated with 'quality of life'. Economic growth had even begun undermining many of the things upon which wellbeing depended, such as responsive democratic institutions, social solidarity, spiritual and aesthetic experience, and stable, functioning ecosystems. The clear implication of these findings was that economic growth should no longer be the primary measure of policy and institutional success in affluent societies; that wellbeing should not be conflated with materialistic success and that, after a surprising low threshold, wellbeing should be sought in non-materialistic realms. But, again, the impact of this line of thinking was essentially non-existent in political and economic circles. Corporate interests – the heartbeat of Empire – ensured that growth economics remained firmly entrenched in the politico-economic realm, and well into the 21st century the reigning orthodoxy was that the answer to almost every problem – including the problems of personal happiness, social justice, and environmental protection – was *more economic growth*. There seemed to be no alternative. So long as most people felt that an increased material 'standard of living' was required to increase 'quality of life', Empire was politically safe.

Unsurprisingly, the legal and political structures of Empire were shaped by this unfettered desire for limitless growth, and those structures both shaped and were shaped by the cultures of consumption that came to define industrial societies. An insatiable craving for more consumer goods and services seemed to animate entire populations. Such commodity fetishism was observable in Western societies from the onset of industrialisation, if not before, but it was really in the decades after the

Second World War when consumption became a truly acute and debilitating social practice. Unmistakably a collective psychological disorder, commodity fetishism reached its zenith at the beginning of the 21st century, establishing a materialistic culture without *any* sense of sufficiency. For reasons which are still not wholly understood, life in these times was structured around the endless pursuit of material luxuries and comforts, and no matter how rich people became, it never seemed to be enough.

During this era the West, in particular, entered a phase of social decay. Despite unprecedented levels of material wealth and sophisticated technologies, most Westerners during these times were working longer hours than they had in the past, and aside from sleeping and working, Westerners generally spent more time watching television than doing anything else. Their diets and lifestyles became highly processed and too often carcinogenic. The division of labour reached an undignified extreme, which may have efficiently maximised growth, but it also meant that people became wholly dependent on the market. People soon found themselves locked upon a consumerist treadmill that had no end and attained no lasting satisfaction. The consumer way of life could not provide many people with a meaningful and fulfilling life. Furthermore, urban sprawl led to highly artificial living environments that disconnected people from a community of neighbours and from any real engagement with nature. This was the hollow culture that transnational corporations celebrated as the ultimate fulfilment of human destiny, the peak of civilisation. But this culture was based on mistaken ideas of freedom, wealth, and happiness, and over time its economy ate away at the natural life-support systems upon which it depended.

It should be noted that counter-cultures certainly existed during this era, offering loud warnings about the social costs and ecological impacts of the global economy. But these oppositional movements ultimately failed to prevent corporate profiteers and consumer cultures from having a devastating and irreversible impact on global ecosystems and biodiversity. Scientists, who used to categorise geological ages into periods of millions of years, began using the term 'anthropozoic' to refer merely to the three centuries following the industrial revolution. During this geological blink-of-an-eye, human economic activity violently degraded the planet in many ways, including pervasive deforestation and the mass extinction of species, climate destabilisation, soil erosion, ocean acidification and depletion, and the overconsumption of many non-renewable resources, most notably, oil.

But would not technology eventually solve all these problems? Despite the zealous faith of technocratic optimists, technology was unable to protect the planet because technological innovation was generally governed by an imperative of growth, not an ethics of sufficiency. This meant that all efficiency gains resulting from technological advancements just went into producing and consuming more, not reducing impact – a paradox first formulated by W.S. Jevons. Technology could not save Empire, because efficiency without sufficiency is lost. By the end of the 20th century it must have been perfectly clear that industrial civilisation had an ecological time limit and that time was running out. But Empire continued to march onward, with wilful blindness, Mother Nature be damned. Needless to say, Mother Nature had ways of dealing with civilisations foolish enough to disrespect her.

As the entire system began to fray, personal and national debts often increased to crippling levels, in an attempt to fund and maintain these destructive, high-consumption lifestyles. The world was greedily borrowing from the future to pay for immediate extravagances, justified on the assumption that future growth would be similar to past growth. But as Rousseau once wrote: 'Civilisation is a hopeless race to discover remedies for the evils it produces'. When the post-war decades of growth came to an end, the world found itself with so much economic and ecological debt that it could not stay afloat. The global economy – like the Titanic of civilisations – began to sink.

Expensive Oil and the Twilight of Growth

In the name of infinite growth, the planet was being stripped bare of its resources. Economists, however, who became chief policy advisors to governments during the 20th century, found little cause for concern. They argued that when certain resources got scarce, prices would go up, providing human beings with incentives to develop substitutes or new technologies. This was the essential market dynamic that economists pointed to when they argued that resources (and therefore the potential for economic growth) were essentially infinite. For present purposes let it simply be noted that at least one critical resource was not easily substitutable – oil – and this biophysical reality was to change the global economy in ways that Empire had not expected.

In order to grow, industrial economies required a cheap and abundant supply of energy, especially oil. Tens of billions of barrels of oil were consumed every year, each barrel of which represented the equivalent of years of embodied human labour. Oil is a finite resource, however, and over the course of the 20th century all the easy-to-find oil was consumed, leaving only the less accessible and lower-grade oils, which were much harder and more expensive to produce. Human beings always pick the low-hanging fruit first. What is more, just as oil supply was tightening, the poorer parts of the world were entering industrialisation, intensifying the competition over the shrinking oil resources. This increasing scarcity and competition made the price of oil go up sharply, but contrary to the theories of economists, oil was not easily substitutable. As a dense source of transportable liquid energy, it turned out oil was essentially unique, meaning that alternatives could not be produced in ways that could control the price. In particular, there was no affordable way to run the world's one billion automobiles without oil, to say nothing of the planes and ships. As for the potential of nuclear energy, it never lived up to its hype, for reasons of expense, insurance issues, social antipathy, and the very real concerns over safety, waste disposal, accidents, and terrorism. Consequently, oil-dependent economies found themselves unable to free themselves from their oil addictions, even though oil was getting increasingly expensive. Naturally, this had consequences.

When the costs of oil increased significantly, this added extra costs to everything dependent on oil, like transport, mechanised labour, plastics, and industrial food production, among many other things. This pricing dynamic sucked discretionary expenditure and investment away from the rest of the economy, causing debt defaults, economic stagnation, recessions, or even longer-term depressions. That was what the world began experiencing early in the 21st century, and it was an economic abyss out of which Empire never emerged. Crude oil production began to plateau while demand was still increasing, and this put huge upward pressure on the price of oil, signifying the twilight of growth economics. The world was not running out of oil, as such, but it had already run out of *cheap* oil. Although very few perceived the significance of all this, humankind soon discovered that it was living at the dawn of a new age.

Expensive oil, in other words, began suffocating the debt-ridden, global economy, bringing an end to three centuries of growth. Unfortunately, mainstream economists, including those in government, seemed oblivious to the close relationship between energy, debt, and economy, and this meant they were unable to see that expensive energy was one of the primary underlying causes of economic stagnation and recession. Consequently, they crafted their intended solutions based on flawed, growth-based thinking, not recognising that the new economics of energy meant that the growth model, which assumed cheap energy inputs, had become dangerously out-dated. When growth-based economies did not grow, households, firms, and nations struggled to repay their debts, and quickly things began to unravel in undesirable ways.

A perfect storm had developed. Acute economic, energy, ecological, population, and cultural problems were crossing paths at the same time, feeding off each other and making the whole even more disastrous than the sum of its parts. The global economy was looking increasingly fragile while at the same time the planet's ecosystems were trembling under the weight of overconsumption. It was only a matter of time before something gave way. It could have been anything.

Ghawar, the Suez Canal, and the Sumed Pipeline

Expensive oil was already suffocating the global economy, in the manner just outlined, when in 2027 one of the world's largest oil fields – Ghawar, in Saudi Arabia – was bombed. Although the Ghawar field was a decade past its production peak, it remained a hugely significant resource in terms of global supply. Within an hour of the first bombing, the Suez Canal and the Sumed pipeline in Egypt were also attacked.

It may have been that expensive oil or ecosystemic collapse was going to bring Empire to an end within a decade or so anyway, even in the absence of geopolitical disruptions. Many were surprised that it had not already fallen. But these bombings proved to be the decisive beginning of the end for Empire – the events that unequivocally initiated the Great Disruption. The attacks were meticulously orchestrated by six young Princeton graduates (four of North American descent, and two of Egyptian descent), all of whom moved to Saudi Arabia after graduating to organise and implement their plan. They crashed two small planes full of explosives into critical areas of the Ghawar oil field, and two similarly loaded planes were crashed into the largest oil refineries nearby. Another plane destroyed an oil tanker on the Suez Canal, and a final plane destroyed a point in the Sumed pipeline. All this caused billions of dollars of damage, but more importantly it upset key supply lines for so long that Empire could never recover.

In an attempt to explain and justify their actions, the six activists left the world a book-length suicide note, entitled 'Lifeblood'. To cut a long argument short, they claimed that Empire had become 'a force of pure evil', one that was 'brutally raping Mother Earth and oppressing the vast majority of humankind for the benefit of a privileged few'. Motivated, they claimed, by 'a fierce love for nature and humankind', they acknowledged the suffering their actions would bring. Nevertheless, on utilitarian grounds, they argued that if Empire were permitted to continue its march, 'the overall suffering of planet and people would be far greater still'. Accordingly, as self-proclaimed martyrs, they gave their lives in the attempt to bring Empire to an end and minimise overall suffering.

Many people believe that there were alternative, less violent, and less disruptive means of bringing about a post-capitalist society, and so castigate these six individuals as 'terrorists' of the highest order. Others feel that only violence could have stopped Empire. Irrespective of one's view, however, it is hard to deny that their plan was exceptionally well formulated, executed, and directed, in the sense that they had the insight to see that Ghawar, especially, was the most exposed Achilles' heel of Empire. With only the six of them involved – only six of them! – these attacks ignited an oil crisis of unprecedented magnitude and endurance, making the price of oil skyrocket at a time when the global economy was already struggling to deal with the impacts of expensive oil and excessive debt.

In the suicide note, the six 'Lifeblood Bombers', as they became known, also claimed that in coming years other groups would execute the bombings of several other oil refineries and supply lines around the world – including the Strait of Hormuz – events that supposedly were already planned. These threats never materialised, however. Many historians today believe that those other bombings were never actually organised, but merely were fabricated threats intended to ensure that oil markets remained high out of fear of further disruptions.

Whatever the case, when the price of oil trebled on the day of these attacks, oil dependent economies realised all at once that the world had changed forever. Without any time to mitigate the impacts of this critical turn of events, the global economy, which had developed three centuries of momentum, hit a wall of steel. It was unable to absorb the impacts of this great, ultimately fatal energy shock.

The party was over.

The Dawn of Deindustrial Civilisation

The declining staircase of Empire was steep and unmerciful. Expensive oil made most international trade uneconomic, meaning that almost overnight nations were faced with the challenge of providing for themselves using only local resources, so far as that was possible. International trade institutions broke down out of redundancy, never to recover. Chronic food shortages provoked political unrest around the world, leading to a series of revolutions, including in the United States, and political boundaries were redrawn, with most large states shattering into much smaller, regional units. Banking and finance systems broke down causing bank runs and chronic deflation throughout the world. Most devastating of all, however, was the resulting population die-off. It would be indecent to state the estimated number of people who perished as a result of Empire's collapse – from starvation, war, and especially disease – but suffice to say that it is well beyond the emotional capacity of human beings to understand.

When looking back on Empire's rise and demise, we see that its progressive development closely resembles a snake eating its own tail, a snake seemingly unaware that it was consuming its own life-support system. In fact, when Empire finally choked on its own way of life, what was surprising was not so much how quickly its existence came to an end, but rather why so few people had foreseen its collapse. For was not collapse the painfully obvious outcome of an economic system whose internal logic was that of limitless growth on a finite planet? If we were to personify Empire and consider it in Freudian terms, we could say that Empire, like Thanatos, had a 'death wish', an unconscious desire to annihilate itself and everything that stood in its way, even Gaia. As we now know all too well, late in the third decade of the 21st century, Empire's death wish was fulfilled by way of the Great Disruption, an event, or rather series of events, that dispassionately throttled the life out of that once mighty economic system, leaving industrial civilisation limp and in tatters, like so many fallen civilisations before it. A stunned and fragmented humanity was left to build new worlds, in whatever ways it could, out of the warm ashes of Empire.

This is the fate we were given, so this is the fate we must love.

3

DEINDUSTRIAL ECONOMY

Industrial civilisation thus became a figment of our historical imaginations. As the period of isolation began, our community on the Isle was left with no option but to begin a new chapter in our story, a chapter in which we had only ourselves and our local resources to rely on. At the same time, we knew that for the foreseeable future our new circumstances would be stamped with the birthmarks of the Old World from whose womb Entropia emerged. Hence the term 'deindustrial economy' came into usage on the Isle, reflecting the fact that our way of life, in both a material and a cultural sense, was situated just over the cliff of industrialisation, not in some distant land where we could create a New World, as it were, out of nothing.

Our industrial heritage is reflected most clearly in our physical infrastructure. Although the original designers of Entropia had aspired to create a radically new society, it is clear that they were never able to escape the industrial paradigm within which they were situated. Rather than experiment with a new type of development, or something other than 'development' altogether, their narrow imaginations merely undertook to do industrial development 'better'. In this limited sense, admittedly, they succeeded in their task: houses and buildings were better insulated; bicycle paths ran alongside every road; and many large parks were inserted amongst the small web of concrete. But it must be said that the early period of Entropia, prior to the crash, was not really an example of an alternative way of life, so much as it was an example of a more egalitarian, happier, and somewhat less impactful form of industrial society. Only when the cargo ships stopped arriving and we realised that our Isle had become the whole world did the embryo of a New World really begin to take form. Even today, in the final year of the 21st century, our deindustrial way of life still seems young. To be sure, we have not yet reached the 'end of history', if that is even a coherent phrase. There will always be more day to dawn.

Another reason our way of life was shaped at birth by industrialisation was the fact that there were considerable stores of industrially produced tools and other material artefacts that obviously remained on the Isle even after industrial civilisation had entered its terminal decline. We may not have had the capability or desire to continue producing such tools and artefacts – at least, not all of them – but we used what the Old World had left us, so far as we found it valuable to do so. We have proven to be diligent caretakers of what today some light-heartedly call our 'industrial antiques'.

Our inheritance, however, does not stop there. Shortly before the Great Disruption a creative group of scientists on the Isle had asked for a shipload of industrial rubbish and consumer trash to be brought to the Isle, for the purpose of experimenting with what they called 'radical recycling'. This group wanted to examine the nature of what industrial civilisation considered 'waste' and to see whether all of this so-called waste could not be re-used productively and creatively rather than sent to landfill. The New Zealand government eagerly responded to this strange request, and promptly dumped vast quantities of rubbish at the processing plant that our community had established near the southeast port. Sorting out and experimenting with these mountainous piles of rubbish provided us with vast quantities of industrially produced materials, such as plastics, metals, fabric, and glass, which, even to this day, we manage to use and reuse for various purposes. Scarcity begets creativity. It is nothing short of astonishing to reflect on what used to be considered 'trash' and how almost all of that trash becomes 'treasure' in an age of material scarcity. The only silver lining to this historic wastefulness was the fact that, as deindustrial civilisation dawned, the rest of the world would also have been able to salvage, as we salvaged, the vast and valuable resources concentrated in the rubbish dumps of what were once called 'consumer societies'. On the Isle, at least, we learned to 'use it up, wear it out, make it do, or do without'.

As it happened, the last cargo ship to arrive on the Isle was the one loaded with consumer waste, and due to a series of significant global disturbances at that precise time, the ship and its crew ended up remaining on the Isle and never leaving. In time the ship was converted into rooms, which today are used for all manner of purposes, from sleeping, to study, to music rehearsals; and since our community has never aspired to leave the Isle, the ship's fuel was drained over time for use elsewhere. Perhaps more than anything else, this trash-bearing cargo ship is the starkest reminder of our industrial history. The huge vessel sits on the southeast harbour like a photograph of a deceased ancestor.

Despite these industrial inheritances, during the seven decades since the Great Disruption our way of life has evolved greatly, almost beyond recognition. No aspect of our life differs from industrial society more drastically than our mode of economy – that is, our practices of production, consumption, and exchange – and since economy lies at the foundation of any society, it makes sense to begin our journey through Entropia by addressing this important subject. As outlined below, the economy we have created is one that has low energy and resource requirements. It aims to provide sufficiently for local needs using local resources, in a way that is ecologically sustainable into the deep future. Given that our community seems to have achieved this ambitious goal, further growth in material wealth is not an economic priority for us. In fact, our economy of sufficiency has been shaped deliberately into a 'stationary state' – that is, an economy that neither grows in terms of energy or resource consumption, nor degrades the natural systems it draws upon. This economy of ours nevertheless provides everyone with the basic material conditions needed to live a full and free life, and therein lies our wealth. As the ancient Chinese philosopher, Lao-Tzu, once said, 'He who knows he has enough is rich', from which it follows that people who have enough, but who do not know it, are poor. Our community's plenitude arises from the fact that we are content with 'enough'.

Notably, we did not need new technological advances to create this way of life. We had everything we needed already, and this shows that Empire's problems did not arise from a lack of technology – which was the common excuse. No, the fundamental problem with Empire was the materialistic, growth-orientated values it adopted when using its technology. When those values disintegrated and we put our existing technologies to the task of ensuring everyone had their basic needs met, we realised all at once that we already had the tools we needed to prosper. Technology is only a means, not an end, and while we are constantly innovating and developing the technologies we consider appropriate, our efforts are driven always by the ethics of sufficiency that define our way of life.

In terms of basic geography, our community is settled on the southwest coast of the Isle, near the mouth of Thalia River. Three small neighbourhoods, each housing five or six hundred people, are situated on the corners of a triangular park, which is about seven hectares in size. This 'central garden', as it is known, serves as the primary social space for our community, as well as being a thriving food forest. As implied above, the original neighbourhoods were designed according to the 'suburban model' of industrial civilisation, and it is within these structures that our new economy has emerged. Farms, orchards, and vineyards lie on the periphery of our settlements, with the rest of the Isle more or less untouched.

♦ ♦ ♦

Water

I will begin the review of Entropia's economy with the issue of water, this being one of the most essential biophysical needs for any form of life. It may sound like a mundane subject, and perhaps it is, but given that our present task is to describe the nature of Entropia's economy, the foundations are where we should start.

The first point to note is that the amount of roof space available to collect rainwater is insufficient to provide our community with all its water needs, modest though those needs are. What this means is that most of the settled areas of the island, including some of the farms, are supported by a mains water system, one not dissimilar to the public service systems that existed in many parts of the Old World. There are also several wells that support the mains system. This infrastructure was established in advance of the first occupation, and for several decades it was required simply to be operated and maintained. In recent years the necessity of our mains system has been highlighted, as rainfall has been much lower than usual, and two of our fossil water wells have dried up.

Despite the mains system on the Isle remaining something close to the industrial system, attitudes to water consumption and collection have undergone a revolution. Whereas domestic consumption in the Old World was typically several hundred litres of water per day, per person, consumption on the Isle has dropped to around 50-70 litres. This is enough for us to live a dignified existence, without leaving much room at all for waste. In those rare cases where a household finds itself consuming much in excess of this, someone in the community who is well versed in methods of water conservation will be invited to advise the household about how best to reduce consumption. These visits are never a matter of moral censure, but simply a matter of social education, and as such they are never resented.

Given that the mains system draws most of its water from various rivers that run throughout the island, it is important that those rivers are treated with the utmost respect. They are, after all, the life-support system upon which the entire community depends, and our motivation to minimise water consumption is based on a commitment to maintain the health and integrity of nature. So deeply engrained is this environmental ethic that it is now just common sense, by which I mean that our practices of water conservation, and conservation more generally, have become habits or rituals carried out almost beneath the level of consciousness. Indeed, the term 'conservationist' has lost much of its meaning today as it no longer has anything from which to distinguish itself. Everyone is a 'conservationist' now, which in a sense means no one is.

In order to draw as little water as possible from the mains system, every household on the Isle has maximised its roof water collection via water tanks. Many large concrete tanks were constructed when the mains system was set up, and various large containers were salvaged from the 'ship of trash' and converted into water collection systems. But generally our domestic water tanks today are constructed from natural materials, such as wood or clay. Despite concrete being extremely energy intensive in construction, however, very occasionally it is still used for making new large community water tanks or piping systems. All things considered, we feel that in such limited circumstances the benefits of concrete outweigh their not insignificant costs, although in time I suspect that the use of concrete will be phased out completely.

Given the importance of water security, essentially everyone on the Isle is proficient in creating and connecting domestic systems of water collection and reuse. Greywater systems are the norm, having been built into the fabric of everyday life. Toilets are flushed, for example, either with tank water or with water collected during showering or cooking. Over time, however, composting toilets (which require almost no water) have come to replace most flush toilets, and this has had particularly significant implications on reducing water consumption. In an age when fresh water is becoming scarcer, the old tradition of directing human waste into drinking-quality water now seems to us not just strange but perverse.

Naturally, tank water is used whenever possible, especially for watering our productive gardens (more on food shortly). Increasingly, households are even establishing domestic 'sand filtration' systems of water purification, to allow tank water to be safely consumed without relying on centralised systems. In those times when we are required to draw from the mains, a little thoughtfulness minimises our consumption. Being conscientious about water consumption when preparing food and cleaning dishes are two areas for conservation, and never watering (or even having) lawns is another. But perhaps the largest savings in the domestic sphere, compared with the Old World, come from how we wash ourselves and our clothes. Generally we wash our clothes less often than was customary in earlier times, but we feel this brings some balance to the Old World's almost obsessive concern with immaculate cleanliness. Furthermore, showering is typically kept to a minute or two, and often people simply wash themselves with a bucket and some soap. This is perfectly adequate as a means of keeping ourselves clean and hygienic. After all, it may be a requirement of a dignified life to clean oneself regularly – achievable if necessary with a bucket of water – but to live well it is not necessary to shower or bathe in the old, water-intensive ways.

Innumerable other water-saving strategies demonstrate that the high water consumption typical of the Old World was really just a product of wastefulness. Certainly, our great reductions have not taken away anything that is necessary for a good and dignified life. So do not pity us, gentle reader! We are richer for our practices of conservation, I assure you. For instance, a culture has developed on the Isle whereby in the warmer months most people bath in the rivers or waterholes, and this not only reduces our dependence on the mains system but it also enriches our lives wonderfully. Just picture the scene of peaceful simplicity! In describing such bathing experiences one can only recall the apt words of Henry Thoreau, who told of how bathing in Walden Pond was a 'religious exercise', providing him with an intense physical and spiritual connection with the natural world. In agreeing with this sentiment I can, of course, only speak for myself, but I suspect my peers on the Isle, most of whom also begin each day with a plunge into the waters of Entropia, would not deny that there is a mystical significance to bathing in the clear rivers or lakes as the sun rises like a warm god over the eastern mount. I am afraid that this mysticism can only be experienced, however, not explained – at least, not explained by me – so for now I will not dedicate any more time to a task to which I suspect mere words could never do justice.

Food

Another foundational issue for any economy is how it obtains and produces its food, and this issue sits next to water on the list of essential needs. Our methods on the Isle are probably most clearly understood by way of contrast to what preceded them, so let me begin there.

The old, industrialised system of food production was grossly unsustainable for various reasons. Not only did industrial farming techniques cause severe and widespread erosion of nutrient-rich topsoil (which takes many hundreds of years to rejuvenate), the industrial system was also extremely dependent on a finite supply of fossil fuels. Natural gas was needed to produce commercial fertilisers, and oil was needed to produce commercial pesticides, to fuel farm machinery, and to create the plastics used in packaging. Most energy-intensive, however, were the exceedingly long supply chains that reached all around the world and which were therefore dependent on oil for transport. Unbelievable though it may sound, in the age of Empire, items in a typical basket of food from a supermarket together could have travelled tens of thousands, or even hundreds of thousands, of kilometres before being consumed. This fossil fuel dependency was highly problematic not only for its horrendous environmental implications, but also because it was economically unsustainable as the price of oil and other fossil fuels became suffocatingly expensive. On top of these issues, the industrialised food system had animal cruelty, distributive injustice, and unspeakable wastefulness built into its very nature. In short, industrial civilisation never had a future because its systems of food production never had a future.

In our deindustrial economy, on the other hand, the systems of food production are local and organic. Ideally these systems would have been voluntarily embraced in advance of the Great Disruption, which would have made the transition thereafter much less taxing, but the early generations struggled to deny themselves the imports of food and oil which they had available to them. When those supply chains abruptly dried up, however, our community found that local and organic farming practices – which in theory we had already embraced – were suddenly forced upon us in practice. Almost overnight we found ourselves unable to rely on imports of any sort – including oil and food – and this necessitated an immediate shift away from energy-intensive systems of food production and importation, toward a system based entirely on local and organic production. While some planning assisted this transition, the reality was that it arose quite spontaneously, for people realised that they had to produce their own food with whatever resources they had, or starve. This experience has some parallels with the 'relief gardens' that arose during the Great Depression during the 1930s and the 'victory gardens' that arose during Empire's second world war. It seems that necessity has always been a great motivator to grow food.

One of the most significant implications of the transition away from industrial food production was the increased labour needed to produce food organically. Environmentalists of earlier ages typically overlooked this issue. While it was widely accepted, even in the industrial era, that organic production tended to be more productive *per acre* than industrial food production, organic production has always been vastly more *labour intensive.* The increased labour requirements arise primarily from the absence of fossil-fuel powered farm machinery, but organic fertiliser production and pest control are also typically more time intensive than industrialised techniques (although several practices can reduce or negate this disparity through strategies like companion planting). What little mechanised farm equipment we do use is powered by our small supply of locally produced, corn-based fuel.

What this means is that organic food production on the Isle was and is entirely capable of feeding our community, but to do so it required a huge increase in the provision of agricultural labour, both human and animal. This was accepted as a necessary implication of the transition away from industrialisation, however it was a transition that also had a large silver lining. Not only did it connect our community more closely with the local land base upon which we all depend for subsistence, but many health benefits flowed from moving away from sedentary forms of labour toward the more active and outdoor work of farming and gardening. However else we may define ourselves on the Isle, we are first and foremost loving stewards of the land that nourishes us.

As well as a proliferation of organic farms on the periphery of our settlements, our economy on the Isle also aims to maximise organic food production *within* those settlements. This happily functions to blur the distinction between town and country. Our productive, home-based gardening began by digging up all lawns and turning them into productive vegetable gardens, and planting fruit and nut trees in all available spaces. Nature strips and other small areas of earth were cultivated; parks were turned into small farms or community gardens; suitable roofs became productive; herbs grow on balconies and windowsills; and generally all food producing potential has been realised. It has even become commonplace for people to cultivate high-protein mushrooms on the shady side of houses and buildings. No growing space is wasted.

Furthermore, most people keep chickens for eggs, bees for honey and wax, and some even keep small livestock, such as goats, for milk and cheese. Animals are also a great source of manure for compost, and primarily for this reason we have built animals into our organic systems. While we found it far too energy intensive to dig up the tar-sealed roads (which were laid down by the original developers of Entropia), we quickly realised the great potential for building raised beds on footpaths and roads; we also discovered that tar-sealed surfaces could be used to collect water. Over the years all this has turned our neighbourhoods into abundantly productive oases, where the freshest food is always within arm's reach, and where children can entertain themselves in the streets and gardens hunting for the ripest plums, almonds, or blueberries.

Productive though our settlements are in terms of food, most people still supplement their domestic production with food produced rurally. This, in fact, is an absolute necessity in most of our quasi-urban contexts, because growing space within those contexts simply does not permit anywhere near strict self-sufficiency. This means that we remain dependent on rural food production and distribution systems. We have three electric trains that serve as supply lines throughout the Isle, and horses and carts are used to bring the food from our small farms to those distribution hubs that sit along the train lines at various points.

Food consumption, not just production, has changed drastically on the Isle. As already implied, our consumption of food is organic and highly localised, and this also means that people eat 'in season', given that we cannot import non-seasonal foods from the other side of the world. Preserving foods in season is our only means of accessing those foods out of season, a practice in which we have become highly proficient. Our food is unprocessed and requires no disposable packaging, since we obtain it either from just outside our backdoors or from our farmers' markets. Although the vast majority of us are vegetarian or vegan, some people still eat small amounts of meat, provided they personally raise and kill the animals themselves, in the most humane way possible. This requirement helps to ensure that people are never distanced from the nature and implications of their food consumption. Our community's small demand for fish and seafood is supplied by some neighbourhood aquaculture systems, supported by a group of fishers who, during strictly limited seasons, cast their rods off the rocks into the lakes and oceans. The trend, however, is towards vegetarianism, and I suspect that meat will disappear from our diets within a generation or two.

Finally, with respect to keeping our soils in good health, we compost human waste for 'humanure' via composting toilets – for use on fruit and nut trees – and we vigilantly compost all our organic food and animal wastes in order to supply our large demand for organic fertilisers. This means none of our so-called organic 'waste' is wasted; it is used to grow more food. Organic matter of all sorts is considered to be of the highest value. One might even say that in our deindustrial economy a good bag of compost is more valuable than a bag of gold – and if people cannot understand that, perhaps they will not understand much about Entropia.

Clothing

With a sufficient supply of water and food secured, the next item on our list of basic material needs is clothing. The primary function of clothing is to keep us warm, and its secondary function, at least in our state of society, is to cover nakedness (although nakedness is no longer the taboo it was in earlier ages). In the Old World the purpose of clothing had evolved to be primarily about expressing one's identity or social status. In Entropia, by contrast, the fashion industry was always considered a superfluous luxury, one costing more than it was worth, and accordingly it never arose. It is worth acknowledging, however, that human beings always have wanted to express themselves through what they wear.

This being so, 'style' did not so much disappear on the Isle, as evolve. A new aesthetic of sufficiency developed, and the old-fashioned expectation to look fashionably 'brand new' is now considered a quirk of history that is incomprehensible to the new generations. Perhaps we look more like the gypsies than anything else that preceded us.

When Entropia was launched all those years ago, the first inhabitants naturally brought with them their own clothing, and indeed most people brought suitcases full of various shirts, pants, dresses, hats, and shoes. Furthermore, much old clothing and fabric was salvaged from the ship of consumer waste, providing further resources for meeting the modest clothing needs in those early days. This meant that systems of clothing manufacture were far from being urgent, as there was a vast stock of existing clothing. It was actually more than a decade before the island was producing any of its own fabrics. Instead of producing new items of clothing, it became customary to wear the pre-existing stock until it was properly worn out, and everyone – man, women, and child – became highly proficient menders and creative 'refashioners'. Some of my earliest and fondest memories are of sitting by the fireside with my grandfather on cold winter evenings, as he would teach me the art of sewing a patch on the knee while telling me stories of the Old World or of Entropia's earlier days. In retrospect, this was where the myths of our culture were born.

Over the longer term, of course, it was not enough simply to reuse, swap, refashion, and mend the original stock of clothing. Eventually we needed to develop systems of production, and in creating these systems our primary aims were functionality and sustainability, not 'profit maximisation' or the pernicious desire for ever-changing styles. Synthetic, petroleum-based fabrics such as nylon and polyester are unknown on the Isle, and cotton generally requires so much pesticide that most of us forgo that otherwise useful fabric too, although we do grow a small amount organically. Instead, functional, easy to grow, low-impact fabrics are used, derived from such things as agricultural hemp, nettles, and wool.

Although these forms of sustainable clothing certainly ended up looking quite different from the stylistic conventions of the Old World, it must be remembered that the consumption of clothing, like all consumption, is a culturally relative social practice, so as more people came to wear second-hand or sustainability designed clothing, new aesthetic standards were established. A time soon came when the idea of wearing 'high fashion' clothing was considered lacking in taste and style, and this cultural shift exemplifies as well as anything the new aesthetics of sufficiency that Entropia has come to represent.

Housing

Describing the nature of housing in our deindustrial economy is a task that demands some subtlety. During the age of Empire, so far as our resources indicate, it seems as if well-meaning 'green' people liked to imagine that the eco-cities of the future were going to look either like some techno-utopia, where everyone was living in million-dollar eco-houses (such as those that used to be glorified in glossy environmental architecture magazines), or else like some agrarian village, where everyone was living in cob houses they built themselves. The fact is, however, that during these long decades following the Great Disruption, our community found itself more or less living in the built environment that was already in existence. We recognised that there were much more resource and energy-efficient ways to construct houses and other buildings, but the poorly designed structures that were in place when the Great Disruption hit were what we had to play with. We were hardly going to knock them all down and start again, just to try to be greener the second time around. In times of crisis people do not care much for idealised blueprints; people make do with what housing they can find, however imperfect it may be. We found that it was important to recognise this reality, and not get too carried away with dreaming of a fundamentally new infrastructure. Recent architectural history on the Isle looks much less romantic, as will the foreseeable future, no doubt.

Rather than dreaming of eco-fairy-tales, the more important and urgent task was to figure out how to make the best of the existing infrastructure. We mended, insulated, shared, reworked, and reconceived – in short, we 'retrofitted' our existing housing stock. It was not always pretty, at least by old-fashioned standards, but we kept warm, dry, and protected, and these of course are the primary functions of a house. We certainly did not spend large amounts of time or resources renovating for purely aesthetic reasons, or extending the house to create a games room. What this means is that, even today, most people on the Isle live in retrofitted houses that existed during the Great Disruption. The possibilities for creative renewal of the existing housing stock are limited only by our imaginations.

As with clothing, however, over time some of the original housing stock is being replaced, and our community has certain expectations about how to do this. Materials are obtained locally, obviously, and our new houses and buildings are designed for long-term durability and to the highest standards of energy efficiency. Owing to the scarcity of metal nails and screws on the Isle, we use hardwood pegs instead, like the Amish, and we practise this technique well. Do remember, however, that replacing the existing housing stock with a long-term, durable alternative will take many, many decades. We have really just begun that process, so if you want to see the agrarian village composed solely of durable, authentically 'green' housing, come and see us in one hundred years or so. For now, most of our houses still look decidedly deindustrial.

When new houses are constructed, they are built much smaller than was typically the case in the Old World, in order to limit the resources required; and they are more densely inhabited. They are in fact very modest – not much like the 'eco-houses' in the old, glossy magazines – but they are sufficient. More than that, in their own simple way they are splendid. Straw-bale and mud-brick houses, as well as various yurts, are becoming more common, and these days most people take part in the construction of their new homes, under the supervision of experts, of course. Our situation has also encouraged creative, less conventional approaches to housing. For example, hundreds of shipping containers, which were used to bring the consumer waste onto the island, have been easily converted into humble abodes; a growing section of the community even chooses to live in large canvas tents or tepees, and in doing so they seem perfectly content with their modest, makeshift dwellings. As noted, our dwellings are mainly clustered together in three small neighbourhoods quite close to each other on the southwest coast, but those who seek more solitude have scattered their huts and cabins all around the Isle.

The radical simplicity and yet sufficiency of our dwellings does raise questions about why people in the age of Empire thought that having such big, ostentatious houses was so important. To again draw on the words of Thoreau: 'Consider first how slight a shelter is absolutely necessary'. Thoreau seeks to remind his readers that while 'civilised' people often spent twenty, thirty, or forty years toiling to pay for their homes, the American Indians of his day lived contently in tepees or wigwams that in the first instance were constructed in a day or two at most, and taken down and put up in a few hours; and every family owned one, or had a place in one. Thoreau even quotes from a man called Gookin, being the superintendent of the Indians subject to the Massachusetts colony, who wrote that 'I have often lodged in their wigwams, and found them to be as warm as the best English houses'. Would the Indians have been wise to give up those wigwams in exchange for the forty years labour required to pay for a more 'civilised' dwelling? The economics of doing so would be dubious, indeed.

In Entropia, where the full costs and benefits of housing are taken into account, people are choosing something far closer to the wigwam than the mansion, and the only problem this presents for us is figuring out how to spend the extra decades of freedom that we did not waste labouring on more 'civilised' dwellings. A delicious problem, if ever there was one.

Energy

I have been proceeding on the assumption that things like water, food, clothing, and shelter are the true necessities of life. But perhaps more fundamental still is the energy needed to secure those things. It is an inescapable law of nature that economic activity requires energy, from which it can be inferred correctly that economic processes are both enabled and limited by energy supply. Energy therefore lies at the heart of all economies, and our economy on the Isle is no different. In terms of energy *demand*, however, the contrast between a growth-based, industrial economy and our non-growing, deindustrial economy could hardly be starker. Whereas the economies of Empire sought as much cheap energy as possible, in the hope of maintaining growth and complexity, our stable, low-consumption economy requires only enough energy to provide a modest but sufficient material standard of living for all. It follows that we have vastly lower energy demands and social complexity, which are the defining characteristics of our way of life.

Prior to the Great Disruption our economy had access to a reasonably secure supply of fossil fuels, and although we recognised that these fuels were finite and ecologically damaging, and that consequently we should be exploring alternatives, our movement away from them was sluggish, at best. It was just too easy to burn the cheap, dense sources of energy, and we kept saying to ourselves that 'soon' we would take renewable energy seriously. But dedicated action was always deferred – and then time ran out.

Fortunately, we had at least directed some of our fossil energy toward establishing systems of renewable energy, so when the crash hit, and the supply of fossil fuel imports came to an abrupt end, we were at least in the process of securing alternative forms of energy. Our small stores of oil and coal were used to fund the transition to renewable sources of energy, and to our credit those stores were dedicated solely to that task. This drew energy away from the rest of the economy, of course, which caused new problems, but because our material needs were so few, we managed to muddle our way through this difficult period without our economy collapsing. Empire, as we know, did not fare so well.

Securing energy is always a context-dependent task. What suits one terrain or climate may not suit another; and the technologies available provide another critical variable. On the Isle, we assessed our circumstances and concluded that hydro and wind were the most appropriate sources of renewable energy for us, and those sources now produce all of our modest electricity supply. We have several water-wheels along Thalia River, and wind turbines of small and medium sizes are scattered throughout and around the vicinity of the neighbourhoods. Although at present we are able to run our electricity grid using metals that existed prior to the Great Disruption, we recognise that in time the wind turbines and the wiring of the grid will need to be replaced, if we are to maintain an electricity supply. Accordingly, we know that we will need to mine for metals at some stage (once recycling existing metal has exhausted itself), so a focus of our research on the Isle is how we are going to mine for necessary metals without using fossil fuels. Our ultimate aim is to create a way of life that can reproduce renewable systems of electricity supply using only renewable energy. Looking into the deep future, if we cannot figure out how to do this, a more primitive way of life awaits us.

Since we do not use fossil fuels, our approach has been to electrify whatever is required for our small economy to function. Given that our supply of electricity is extremely tight, however, human and animal labour is still our default mode of energy until a case can be made for electrification. One exception, as I have already mentioned, is our modest production of corn-based oil that we use to power some farming machines and light vehicles in limited circumstances. Our hydro and wind systems are also supplemented by wood fuel, which some households burn for heat to cook with or when the winters get especially cold. There is an area just northeast of our settlement that is dedicated to growing wood for fuel and housing, and we strictly adhere to the principle that every tree we cut down must be replaced. This is just one of many ways that we protect ourselves against meeting the same fate as the Easter Islanders.

Unfortunately we have not yet developed very successful ways of storing energy. Currently, when energy supply exceeds demand, we pump water to an upper reservoir, thus storing potential energy through gravity, and run that water downhill through a wheel generator when the energy is required. This is not a particularly efficient method of storage, but it suffices for our low-energy society. When the wind is not blowing, however, we sometimes find that our demand for electricity exceeds supply. Nevertheless, we have come to prepare for and adapt to these situations well, and we now accept that occasional supply disruptions are a relatively small price to pay for living in a post-carbon economy.

Transitioning to a post-carbon economy, however, was not just about transitioning to renewable energy systems and otherwise continuing 'business as usual'. An economy is not sustainable merely because it runs on renewable energy; the economic activity itself must be sustainable, which is the problem the growth-based economies of Empire would have faced even if they had managed to transition to renewable energy. A rainforest does not regrow any faster just because it was cut down with tools charged by renewable energy instead of oil; nor would the forest's biodiversity suffer any less on that basis. In short, sustainability demands both sustainable ends and sustainable means, a lesson that we have slowly come to learn.

What we have discovered is that running an economy solely on renewable sources implies having much less energy to play with. It just was not practicable for us to produce the same amount of energy from renewable sources as we had been producing with fossil fuels. So as well as fundamentally rethinking our *production* of energy, we had to fundamentally rethink our *consumption*. This led to all manner of lifestyle changes aimed at minimising energy usage, some of which were challenging, but most of which were not. For example, in the warmer months most of us shower under water heated by the sun (or, as I have said, we just clean ourselves in the river); and on every sunny day we cook with solar ovens rather than draw electricity from our tiny grid by using our electric stoves. We also wash our clothes by hand and dry them on washing lines, and more generally, we do without most electronic technologies or replace them with manually operated ones. We do not have computers or televisions, and we get by just fine. In the colder months of winter we even find that we can turn our fridges off and just store our food in cool spaces (and many households have begun changing their diets to extend this period). If our bodies are cold, we will always layer up with wool before thinking of turning on our electric heaters or lighting a fire. Humans are hardier than they sometimes think they are.

Undoubtedly the most significant reason for our low energy consumption however is the fact that we have minimal need for mechanised transport. Given that our economy is a local economy, no energy is spent shipping, trucking, or flying goods all around the world; when materials and people need to be moved around the Isle, we use our electric trains or our very small fleet of communally owned light vehicles, which run on biofuels. Whenever possible we use bicycles or even the old-fashioned horse and cart, which might seem quaint to those who lived in the age of the automobile but it suits us fine. Certainly, nobody ever needs to drive a vehicle to work, because again our economy is structured so that we all live near our place of work or along a bicycle path or train line (and often we work productively in our own homes, an issue to be addressed further shortly). These and countless other lifestyle choices and conservation efforts mean that our energy consumption is only a small fraction of the levels reached in the so-called 'developed nations' of Empire.

The ultimate lesson of energy is this: a society must adapt to its sustainable energy supply if it is to prosper over the long term. If it does not adapt to that energy supply – that is, if it tries to maintain ever increasing social and technological complexity by forever increasing its energy supply – it will eventually exceed its energy supply and collapse. Historically, civilisations have always attempted to maintain growth and complexity by expanding energy supply, not realising that there comes a point when the social and ecological costs of growth and complexity exceed their benefits. At such a point, voluntary simplification is the most appropriate response, even if it is a response that inevitably demands deep societal adjustment and reorientation. In Entropia, we showed the wisdom to choose voluntary simplification rather than unsustainable growth and complexity; that is, we created a stationary, post-growth economy based on a culture of simple living. By virtue of that, our way of life now has the potential to flourish into the deep future.

Work and Production

As well as the truly revolutionary transformation that took place in terms of energy, our deindustrial economy can also be understood with respect to the fundamental changes that took place in terms of work and production. The most significant of these changes was that the household again became a place of production, not merely consumption. This transition was driven partly by choice, but in the very tough economic times following the Great Disruption we found that home production was often more of an economic necessity. Rather than hiring other people to grow our food, cook our meals, make our clothes, build our furniture, look after our children, maintain our houses, etc., generally we have come to take care of such things ourselves. At the same time, households often produce goods for trade or barter, such as furniture, pottery, clothes, or food, and thereby contribute to the local economy through this home production. Artisans also produce speciality goods at the household level, such as musical instruments, paintings, or various tools.

It was not so long ago, we must remember, when these forms of home production were the norm. Unfortunately, home production in the age of Empire rarely received the respect it deserved. In fact, it was an unfortunate consequence of the women's rights movement that home production was often denigrated. When women were forced through cultural expectations to be the 'home-maker' while men went out and ran the formal economy and governed the nation, it was perfectly understandable why the liberation of women seemed to imply leaving the home, joining the formal workforce, and outsourcing home production. But the importance of being given equal freedoms should not have implied, as it too often did, that staying at home was somehow a sign of oppression or failure. There is honour in home production, provided it is not imposed upon one gender involuntarily. In Entropia, I am happy to report, home-based production (whether undertaken by women or men, or both) is recognised for what it is – the heart of any economy.

This should not, however, be understood to mean that we attained or even aspired to strict self-sufficiency at the household level. In most cases, that would be neither desirable nor possible. Much of our production still takes place beyond the household, but the nature of what is produced and the values motivating production are very different from earlier times. We have discovered that we can produce many of the things we happen to desire from industrial civilisation, including plastics (derived from cellulose), *provided the scale of production is vastly reduced.* Nevertheless, the provision of basic needs – such as food, clothing, shelter, tools, and medicine – is the primary focus of our production, and our defining motivation is to produce what is necessary and sufficient for a good life, rather than to produce luxuries or superfluous abundance. While some factories remain in order to provide certain materials and technologies (such as light bulbs, paper, building and gardening equipment, wind turbines, bicycles, etc.), small private enterprises and worker cooperatives have replaced the mega-corporation. The local grocer and hardware store have returned to Mainstreet, and community owned-and-operated farms provide much of our community's sustenance.

Given that the levels of consumption on the Isle are radically lower than was common in consumer societies in the Old World, it is worth emphasising that the levels of production are considerably lower too. This implies reduced working hours for most of us – in the formal economy, at least – creating far more time for leisure and the necessary home production. One consequence of this is a blurring of the distinction between work and leisure, as people spend far more time working on their livelihoods at home, at their own pace and in their own way. It is also worth reiterating, however, that in some respects – such as food production – much more labour is required, due to the absence of fossil fuel use in production. In our economy, a far greater proportion of us work as farmers than in the Old World, but far from being a regressive step, this is generally considered a positive advance away from office or factory work. People are working outdoors with their hands in the soil, once again connected with the natural systems upon which our most basic needs depend.

Money, Markets, and Exchange

The question of what role money, markets, and exchange play in our economy is complex. Nevertheless, as I bring this exposition of our economy to a close, some broad comments must be made on these important subjects. First of all, it is worth noting that throughout history, human beings have exchanged goods and services with each other, either by way of barter, gift, or through the use of money. These practices continue in our economy, although the nature of money, markets, and exchange has evolved greatly, as have our attitudes toward them. As noted above, our economy does not demand that everyone (or anyone) is strictly self-sufficient. Households are as self-sufficient as possible, but there are still 'markets' for various goods and services that cannot be produced or undertaken within the household. A basic monetary system remains the most convenient tool for 'keeping accounts', so to speak, but non-monetary forms of exchange, such as gift and barter, have become much more prominent modes of economic activity.

Since profit-maximisation is not the aim of market activity in Entropia, less attention is given to producing things that fetch the highest price, and more attention is given to producing what the community most needs. A community-run bank was set up early on, which oversees the monetary system and provides zero-interest credit for projects the community deems necessary or appropriate. This system is required to maintain our stationary state economy. There are certainly no privately operated banks that offer interest-bearing loans, for that would lay the foundations for a growth economy, which we have categorically rejected.

The formal economy, so to speak, takes place primarily on Mondays and Thursdays, and every second Saturday, when the various markets are set up. These market days provide more than enough time for people to obtain whatever they might need for the week. It also means that people only ever work two or three days in the formal economy, leaving the rest of the week to relax or get creative in the studio, workshop, study, or garden. The market days are vibrant, social, and colourful community events, where our musicians gather to showcase their latest compositions while people wander the various stalls and stores.

The fact that markets of some variety still remain on the Isle implies correctly that some forms of private property endure, although it is also the case that since the Great Disruption more of the economy has come under social control – a political issue we will examine in more detail in a later chapter. I should note, however, that the term private property is somewhat misleading here, given that our property system, so far as it exists, barely resembles anything that preceded it. A good economy must be designed so that everyone has 'enough', and this means that communities have to take responsibility for ensuring that basic needs are universally met. This requires a significant degree of social control of the economy, in the sense at least that the provision of basic needs for all is considered a social responsibility that cannot be left to market forces. It also demands some sensible limits on accumulation, especially in a non-growing economy. While strict equality is not enforced on the Isle, we recognise that significant disparities of wealth are socially corrosive and politically dangerous.

The most important issue, we feel, is that everyone has access to arable land and the means to support themselves and their families, for this means that people are never under economic duress to accept degrading work on unjust terms. While most people on the Isle are self-employed or work as part of a cooperative, should someone ever be without work then the community is the employer of last resort, as there is always important work to be done. Consequently, our society knows no unemployment and no destitution; on the contrary, we all have enough and know we have enough.

Thus, in our simplicity, we are rich.

4

FLOURISHING IN SIMPLICITY

Having been introduced to the basics of our economy, readers will have questions, no doubt, about the political nature of our simple living community and how we govern ourselves. The short answer is that we practise a form of participatory democracy, based on radically egalitarian ideals, through which everyone is expected to play some role in social governance. Before discussing political issues, however, I feel it is important to provide a deeper insight into the nature of daily life on the Isle, for until that is better understood, any discussion of our community's politics would be somewhat premature, like putting a cart before the horse. A political system can be no better than its culture, even if politics both shapes and is shaped by its culture. In this chapter, then, I will endeavour to illustrate the culture of Entropia and our simpler ways, drawing on my own experiences as well as some writings from my peers. I hope that this puts some more intimate flesh on the descriptive bones of the last chapter, and goes some way to showing why life on the Isle is good, despite the very humble nature of our material circumstances.

♦ ♦ ♦

I have already mentioned that our housing stock is deindustrial in nature, in the sense that we have retrofitted our suburban-style neighbourhoods, rather than built an entirely new village of mud-brick houses. In order to shed more light on our way of life, however, perhaps I could invite you into my neighbourhood for a closer look around. Although every abode on the Isle has become charmingly unique through creative adaptation to our deindustrial circumstances, there is a sense in which my residence is as representative as any, and it is naturally the one I know best. It is also a source of considerable pride and pleasure for me, modest though it is, so I would be delighted to show you around.

My residence is situated in the neighbourhood closest to the western beach. Picture a tiny settlement of roughly one hundred houses in a relaxed coastal village. At last count there were just shy of six hundred inhabitants in this neighbourhood, all of whom know each other by name. Most houses on the Isle are single-storey, wooden or brick bungalows, although in each of the three neighbourhoods there is a central, four-storey apartment-style block that is home to about one hundred people. Six short, tar-sealed, cul-de-sacs radiate from those central blocks, with houses, yurts, and shipping-container homes nestled in amongst our flourishing gardens and orchards. I live in one of the wooden bungalows, with my partner, another couple, and three children whom we raise, not communally, but with many shared responsibilities. This makes for a busy, densely inhabited household, which is the norm, but that is the way we like it, and indeed, that is the way it must be.

As there are only three bedrooms in the house, the three young children currently share a room, but our household is in the process of building a small, mud-brick 'shed' in the backyard, anticipating a time when another bedroom will be required as the children grow up. The shed is proving to be quite a labour-intensive project, even for such a little construction, but it is very satisfying to be so intimately involved in building our own shelter. It seems like a very human thing to do, even if it was a pleasure lost to so many in the Old World.

Inside our bungalow, minimalism is the governing philosophy; at least, we do our best to follow William Morris' advice to have nothing in our house that we do not 'know to be useful, or believe to be beautiful'. The bedrooms, in particular, are sparsely furnished, and not cluttered with superfluous stuff. The beds originally lay on significant wooden bases with large headboards, but all of them now lie on very low bases without headboards, a result of our household needing to find spare wood to build ourselves a desk for the lounge and a small table for the kitchen. Throughout the house our old carpet has worn thin, but recently we acquired flax mats from the market to cover the worst areas. These mats can be taken outside easily and shaken, which is ideal given that we do not have a vacuum cleaner. Shoes are left at the door.

The paint on the walls is in a similar state of wear, with numerous chips and scratches commemorating a history of active living. But far from offending our aesthetic sensibilities, we feel this just adds character. In any case, interior paint is not easily acquired on the Isle, and never for merely cosmetic purposes. Our couches, chairs, tables, and clothes lack any consistent aesthetic style – we are happy to acquire what we need, when we can – but functionally they are without fault. In much the same way, the old jam jars that our household uses as cups serve the required purpose very well, making the scarcity of conventional glasses no problem at all. These types of creative adaptation give rise to a unique, deindustrial feel to our way of life, which we have come to accept and even enjoy. It certainly reminds us that the old, consumerist imperative to have everything looking consistently 'brand new' must have been a terrible and costly burden. Thankfully, those days are well and truly gone.

This brief description, I fear, might give the impression that our house looks like part of a run-down, derelict ghetto, but I must emphasise that this is far from the case. Our couches and armchairs might be old and worn, but they are covered with bright, homemade woollen throws of elaborate design, and on cold winter evenings in front of a wood burner, they are the most inviting places in the world. Humble beauty and homeliness are all around us. On our walls in the small kitchen, above the stove, hang several exquisite sketches and watercolour paintings of the Isle's sublime scenery and wildlife, which were gifted to us by our neighbour who is a prolific and well-respected artist. In the lounge hang a revolving series of mostly colourful, abstract works, produced within our own walls, all of us being passionate amateurs. These bright paintings complement the thick maroon and navy curtains, hanging from the northern windows, which might otherwise have been an eyesore. We make the best of what we have.

A fine wooden sculpture of Epicurus sits prominently above the fireplace, between two shelves of old books, under which is inscribed his words: 'Do not spoil what you have by desiring what you do not have'. In the centre of the lounge, three black lanterns sit on the low, redwood table, providing us with a soothing ambience on those evenings when we have friends over to share a meal or play some music. The desk in the corner, which we made out of the bed bases and headboards, is a source of considerable pride to us all, and it shows more than a little craftsmanship, if I may say so. Upon the table sits a treadle sewing machine, which symbolises the creative spirit and appropriate technology that define life within our simple yet productive abode. As will be clear, our house certainly lacks 'modernist chic', but it is warm, bright, and creative, and it is the place we call home. It might not be much, but it is enough, and just enough is plenty.

Like every backyard on the Isle (and front yard for that matter), ours is a productive array of vegetable gardens, fruit trees, compost heaps, chicken coops, bee hives, and water tanks. Gardening is a regular part of life for everyone on the Isle, from the youngest to the oldest, with everyone playing their part, absorbing or imparting the wisdom of ages. The fourteen raised garden beds in our backyard are made from the fence that used to demarcate our section from our neighbours – a boundary that is now happily blurred and increasingly irrelevant. Grape and passionfruit vines scale the northern and western walls of the house. In our neighbours' backyard there is a formidable hardwood table, at which our immediate community regularly gathers for shared meals, and occasionally for larger gatherings of friends. Woven throughout the neighbourhood is a maze of walkways, creeks, bridges, and ponds, and everywhere saunterers can find quiet, enchanting sanctuaries to sit, read, or meditate, or just have a short afternoon siesta in the serenity of our garden paradise.

A passage from a friend's journal – her name is Laura Jane – provides a fair snapshot of our simpler ways of living:

> *Sunday morning, after tuning the piano and having a short practice, I took a stroll along the beach, and even braved the cool waters. I didn't last long though! Too cold, despite the sun. On my way home, refreshed by the swim, I passed through Haley's garden to find her two grandchildren sitting on the edge of a garden bed, podding and eating peas, while deep in conversation about this or that. I passed by silently with a smile, not wanting to interrupt their happy business. Closer to home I came across Haley's brother, Hayden, who proudly told me he had turned 'eighty-three years young' the day before. I sat with him for a while on an old bench overlooking a pond.*

He played the ukulele and sang soulfully to an audience of dragonflies, with a husky but tuneful voice. Enriched by his musical tales, which were full of poetry, wisdom, and verve, I made my way back home, where I bottled some pears in the afternoon with Caleb, and did some preparatory reading for tomorrow's classes. I worked a little on my novel – I'm not sure it's any good, but I'm loving the process – and I mended a hole in my favourite sweater. In the evening, I met up with a group of friends in the central garden, near Walnut Grove, where we sipped on some homemade port and threw ideas around about organising a series of dawn plays in the summer. I strolled home just before midnight, a light, misty rain moistening the air. I took a moment to acknowledge the hedgehog whose path I was fortunate enough to cross, and in the distance I heard the laughter of a dinner party that was obviously reluctant to end. As I walked up the stairs of my front porch I saw the gutter that needed fixing – must get onto that before class tomorrow.

Life on the Isle is peaceful, no doubt, but I do not wish to give the impression that it is all singing and siestas. We work hard – very hard, I would say – but the work is meaningful and dignified, so our busyness is not something to be lamented. First of all, our expansive gardens do not tend themselves, and even if they did, I doubt we would spend any less time with them, gardening being so good for the soul. There always seems to be work to do, weeding here and there, maintaining this or that. There is always compost to turn, seedlings to plant, or firewood to chop, and if it is raining there will be clothes to mend, food to prepare, or study to be done. Beyond one's own households, our broader neighbourhoods also require constant maintenance and care, whether that involves pruning our productive trees in the central gardens or collecting their produce, fixing a bridge or gate, helping paint the town hall, organising the market days, mending a community cart or bike, feeding the animals or cleaning their pens, and so forth. Good honest peasants' work, but with the distinct advantage that we have no monarch to whom we must answer! No wonder so many people hum a tune while they work. The necessary work gets organised in a variety of ways – sometimes through spontaneous volunteering and sometimes through slightly more formal 'working bees', but should an important job find itself neglected, there are regular neighbourhood meetings where such issues are raised and generally resolved, either through volunteering or invitation.

There is, of course, more formal employment in which we are all engaged. Currently, most people work around fifteen hours per week in the formal economy, a number that rises and falls depending on need (or desire), but which has been relatively stable in recent decades. We obviously work many more hours in the informal economy: gardening, cooking, cleaning, mending, building, raising children, and so forth. Like most people, I have more than one job. I am a part-time lecturer at the Academy, as noted earlier, as well as an assistant editor of a local newspaper, called *The Saunterer*, which is community owned and operated. The diversity of employment keeps life interesting, and if a job loses its attraction, it is usually possible to transition to something more suitable in a reasonable timeframe. I also bind books as a hobby, taking pride in my craft, and this earns me a little extra money at the market, or provides a service or product that allows me to barter for those few things I might need. On Tuesdays I also work on one of the farms just beyond our settlement, picking fruit and tending to the crops. In this diversity, I am typical, even if the details will be unique to each individual.

As well as these types of employment, there is an array of worker cooperatives, guilds, and sole practitioners that provide for the variety of economic needs on the Isle, whether goods or services. Most people work their way through various professions, trades, or crafts in a lifetime, although there are also many people who aspire to master one speciality or advance a specific discipline, focusing their life upon it. Depending on one's skills and interests, a person finishing school might become a potter, a carpenter, a builder, a baker, a farmer, a blacksmith, a music teacher, a lecturer, a tailor, a doctor, or some mixture of such roles. There is also a need for people to specialise in the social services and utilities, such as building wind turbines and water wheels, or maintaining the plumbing, electricity, and train systems. There is a volunteer association which meets monthly to explore whether new products, services, or technologies might be appropriate and desirable for the Isle, and their findings are published in my newspaper. This provides some guidance on what areas might need to be filled in the economy, or whether some cooperative ventures in existence could be phased out. This way our labour remains efficient.

It should be clear from this overview that our economy, to borrow Marx's words, is one 'where nobody has one exclusive sphere of activity but each can become accomplished in any branch [he or she might wish]', making it possible 'to do one thing today and another tomorrow, to hunt in the morning, to fish in the afternoon, rear cattle in the evening, criticise after dinner... without ever becoming a hunter, fisherman, shepherd or critic'. The point deserving of most emphasis, however, is that genuine fulfilment comes from finding varied and suitable employment under non-coercive conditions. To be sure, there is no 'curse of labour' in our community. The best way to think of working life on the Isle is to think of the craftsperson or artisan who is enriched by the creative process of labouring, and who finds great satisfaction in bringing their productive projects to fruition through the exercise of their skill. By keeping our material needs simple, work does not become oppressive or drudgery. Even the less attractive jobs, such as cleaning toilets or shovelling manure, do not seem so bad when they are shared amongst all members of the community, rather than forced upon an underclass. On the Isle, no one is 'above' such work.

Owing to our passion for life, our community generally rises with the sun. We do this partly because there is always so much life to live – so much interesting and important work to be done. But it also means that our waking hours are naturally illuminated by the sun, thereby minimising our need to use energy for lighting in the evenings. This is but one of infinite examples of how our way of life flows according to natural and seasonal rhythms. In another sense, however, the Isle never sleeps. There will always be people engaged in creative activity throughout the night, in the libraries, workshops, and studios, resisting sleep for the sake of staying absorbed in their work. When a muse happens to be inspiring someone, our community does its best to provide the fortunate artist or artisan with the time and space they need to channel their inspiration, and if this means an individual must stay up until the sun rises, and arrive late to the cooperative meeting in the morning, or not at all, then generally we find ways to accommodate these occurrences, or plan for them in advance. It would be a terrible shame to miss out on a delightful tune, a fine sculpture, or an enriching poem for the sake of a meeting! All of us would be the poorer for it.

By maximising people's opportunity to engage in creative activity, the Isle is awash with the most thrilling novels, plays, poems, music, sculpture, paintings, tapestries, and all other forms of art, beyond historical precedent and beyond historical imagination. What is more, our artistic expressions have become so infused into the fabric of daily life that it could be said that the distinction between art and life has collapsed. The result is that the relationship between human beings is no longer the old, stagnant relationship of lord and serf, or capitalist and worker, or producer and consumer, as it was in the age of Empire, but has become the revolving, mutually respectful relationship of artist and art-lover. If in no other way, life on the Isle is justified as an aesthetic phenomenon.

All this means that the distinction between work and leisure has more or less disappeared too. We rarely crave the end of the working day, nor is our leisure unproductive and passive. In fact, often it is not clear whether a person is at work or play. We may seem 'poor in things', according to the standards of the Old World, but we are 'rich in time', in the sense that we have ample time for the things in life that matter most to us – whether that be work, art, family, study, social life, or something else. It is the engagement of those meaningful activities that keeps us busy, but should we feel the need for a quiet cup of tea under a tree at any time during the day, whether to read a book or simply listen to the birds, then that is something that can be easily indulged. Consequently, life on the Isle moves as fast or slow as the moment requires. In short, we seem to have found the elusive balance of which the old philosophers spoke. As John Ruskin once wrote: 'There is no wealth but life'.

One important consequence of our simpler way of living is the beneficial side effects it has on health. On this subject I can do no better than quote from a recent study led by one of our doctors of medicine, Dr Simone de la Porte, who summarises her team's analysis as follows:

> *This study explores the health implications of 'simple living' and compares this way of living to earlier 'consumerist' lifestyles. The available evidence shows*

that consumerist lifestyles, as exemplified in western societies of the Old World, tended to be associated with highly processed diets and obesity, a lack of exercise, a disconnection from nature and community, as well as elevated levels of stress, anxiety, and substance abuse. These practices led to unprecedented levels of what might be called 'the diseases of affluence', such as heart disease, cancer, diabetes, high blood pressure, and depression.

But rather than reconsider the lifestyles that caused these illnesses, healthcare in the Old World sought to cure these illnesses with pills and technologies, which could be commoditised and sold for a profit. An alternative approach was to prevent those illnesses through lifestyle changes, which would have been essentially free. We argue that the 'commoditisation' approach followed logically from the capitalist nature of the Old World, which was structured to privilege profit above people. In short, selling people pills was more profitable than advising patients to change their lifestyles, thus marginalising preventative, lifestyle medicine.

The 'commoditisation' approach contrasts sharply with the 'lifestyle' approach to healthcare as practised on the Isle. Our empirical research shows that the lifestyles of moderate consumption on the Isle have a range of health benefits, flowing from our unprocessed, vegetarian or low-meat-consumption diets, our active, outdoor lifestyles, our close connection with nature and community, as well as our work-life balance. Not only is this important from a personal perspective, healthy living means less burden on community health systems, freeing up more funds and resources for other causes. This study provides an empirical basis for the notion that the best way to live a long, healthy, low-impact life, is to live simply.

Healthy though we are, it would be a mistake to think that this means we are puritanical in our consumption. Most things are problematic if consumed in excess, just as most things are unproblematic if consumed in moderation. On that basis we sometimes enjoy, without abusing, the sensual pleasures of alcohol and various other intoxicants, and certainly find no justification for restricting people's liberty in relation to such substances. When people are of mature age, properly educated, and in a community of friends, we find that a libertarian policy on intoxicants is the most appropriate approach. We consume these things, I should add, not because we feel the need to 'escape' from our lives. It is just biophysically the case that the consumption of certain roots, leaves, herbs, fungi, and flowers, etc., can have pleasurable and sometimes mind-expanding effects on the human consciousness, which is why intoxicants such as alcohol are as old as civilisation. As we like to jest: 'Everything in moderation – even excess!'. On summer evenings, for example, around a campfire on the beach, it can be quite pleasant indeed to pass round a bowl of kava – the roots of which produce a drink that induces a relaxing state of mild euphoria, without disrupting mental clarity. Sometimes we talk, sing, and dance ourselves into the night, only to fall asleep on the beach and wake to the sunrise and dawn chorus. Pleasure can be an end in itself; it just must not be mistaken to be the only end.

We are similarly relaxed in our attitudes toward sex and relationships. Although something resembling the nuclear family remains the basis of our society, relationships are as open or closed, so to speak, as the people involved desire them to be. Monogamy may not be for everyone, but honesty and respect are. As such, the expanded relationships that sometimes form on the Isle raise no eyebrows and certainly draw no moral censure, although they no doubt would have shocked the old middle-classes of Victorian morality. In this sense, it might be said, we are libertine.

As for marriage, the institution has faded away. In historic times when women were dependent on men for economic security, the legal bind of marriage helped provide that security, although it also functioned to commodify the woman as the man's property. In later times, marriage served to denote 'legitimate' relationships and marginalise 'improper' relationships, according the prevailing bourgeois ethics. Naturally, we do not sympathise with these features of marriage, including the assumption that a 'legitimate' relationship can only be between man and women. For us, sexual orientation is solely a matter of individual preference, and we cannot understand what all the fuss used to be about. Love is love, is it not? Our culture accordingly ushered the institution of marriage into history. This is not to say that a great deal of historic marriages were not based on a great deal of love. It is only to acknowledge that the institution carried a lot of baggage – baggage we chose to leave behind. Nevertheless, most people still passionately commit themselves for life to someone, declaring that love from the rooftops, and weaving their lives together as one. It is only that we choose not to institutionalise that love. Perhaps it is the anarchist in us, but we do not feel we should need a piece of paper from a state to authenticate or legitimatise something so intimate. Celebrating a life together does that just fine.

If I have given the impression that our community resembles a freethinking and somewhat hedonistic faction of the Amish, who have established for themselves a New Bohemia of simple living, poet-farmers, then perhaps I have done justice to the truth. I say this only somewhat tongue-in-cheek.

♦ ♦ ♦

Let me tell you now about one particularly memorable happening on the Isle, which is merely a story of simplicity. It took place a couple of years ago, as the slowly setting sun marked the beginning of the Midsummer's Night Festival. It was a warm, glorious evening, and most of the community, including myself, had gathered outdoors in the Grecian amphitheatre, awaiting the opening ceremony in a mood of relaxed excitement. There was a thunderous crash of a gong, suggesting an imminent commencement, and the crowd hushed in anticipation. Francesca Blake, one of our most beloved and affirming poets, took to the twilit stage and paused for a moment, a solitary figure beneath a low sun and a high moon. When there was perfect silence, she began to speak:

> *A respected elder of a small town in the Old World is strolling one spring evening in the woods. While circling close to the shores of a secluded pond he crosses paths with an apparently disaffected romantic poet, but one who seems temporarily in the mood for society. As the sun calmly ushers itself from the scene, the following civil confrontation takes place. I give you: 'Invitation / Incitation'.*

At this point Francesca left the stage to be replaced with two others: Jeremiah, who bowed and introduced himself as 'the Elder', and Fredrico, who bowed and introduced himself as 'the Poet'. After positioning themselves on separate sides of the stage and waiting a moment, the Elder slowly walked over and engaged the Poet in conversation:

Elder:

Citizen poetic,
I find deliberately astray,
You seem a being without having,
As if having didn't pay,
Wild mystical enigma,
Is the state of your inside,
It has you even as I speak,
Devouring yourself alive.

Expecting tranquillity in gentle soliloquy,
Through wandering woods to this pond,
I left my business alone in the township this eve,
In search of what might lie beyond,
Yet no surprise should it have been,
This far from good society,
That I cross upon a militant romantic,
Of some quiet crossbred variety.

Are you one of those who propose in revolt,
'Find your path that simplicity has broken'?
Don't tell me that you're an inciter of this!
Perhaps we should never have spoken,
I tend to tire of such romance, you see,
Please forgive me my honesty here,
A life lived imagining some 'Other' to gold,
Would explain your kaleidoscope stare.

With eyes of infinite affirmation,
To each their own black hole,
They glisten with free spirit,
And leak of radioactive soul,

Still something in their glow sings,
In melancholy keys,
The tune is of a mind gone diving,
Far too deep for me.

But enough of my impressions,
Which so rudely forth I spew,
I'll bid you now good evening, sir,
And leave you to your view,
Unless of course a bard you are,
Without a place to be?
In which case might you fight twilight,
Inciting verse with me?

Poet:

Witness O mysterious other,
Who wanders in from beyond,
Like mist emerging from the woods,
To settle on the pond,
With etiquette poetic,
Charm refined without pretence,
You seem a gentlemanly brother,
With many dollars, but fewer cents.

As for me a place to be,
Is none but than right where I am,
Passing through in awe,
What commerce cannot understand,
You could too see through this worldview,
If you saw what yours ignores,
Please don't be quick to think I'm lost,
For simply wandering these shores.

Just bathe your eyes in these soft ocean skies,
Of blue, purple, and pink,
And you will find in this sublime,
That there are worse places to sink –
Crass rat race, not to my taste,
Out from the rush I stepped with haste,
It gave me twisted faces,
Only here I find my grace.

A welcome cosmic accident,
Of time and chance I trust,
That we should meet this setting sun,
Among all Nature in the dusk,
So come and join my meditations,
Burning in the dew,
Tonight I'd like to fight twilight,
Inciting verse with you.

A discourse did ignite,
Two lanterns on a kite,
Which we cast out at darkness,
To carry forth light,
This may lead us past yonder,
But before we go too far,
Perhaps you would tell me,
Who on earth you are?

'Who are you?' it is asked of me,
With a seriousness hitherto unseen,
Please may we start with an easier question,
Or next you'll ask me what I mean.

'Tis best methinks you evaded the subject,
Because now my suspicion is this,
If you tried to tell me the truth of your meaning,
You'd never stop changing the script,
So rather than bother you and cause you the trouble,
To live only a life of review,
Agreed we should start with an easier question,
Why not just tell me what you do?

On the far side of the shore,
Beneath a tree there sits a chair,
Where I front every morning star,
With questions God is meant to hear,
Then later in the day,
Like a mad Dostoyevskian clown,
I chase my butterfly thoughts fragmented,
And try to write them down.

With your ink among the birds,
A sojourner in search of words,
In this strange way to spend your day,
Have you found something new to say?

I have yet found but few new words,
In this sense I'm a flightless bird,
So destiny has me,
Repeating only things I've heard:
– Just enough is plenty –
– Abundance is a state of mind –
Since this can cure the Golden Plague,
My fate is not part-time.

So will you quietly revolt?
This is my soul refrain,
Like Abraham, if you give up,
You'll get more back again,
Compose yourself a simple life,
The poet's leap of faith,
At the edge of the abyss,
Creation seems to be at stake.

Come, let us foresee the starry night,
That perfect economy,
Alone, together,
In silence.

The crowd in the amphitheatre remained silent. We were all waiting for the next turn in conversation, eager to hear more. But as the silence persisted it dawned upon us that silence was the point. Unknowingly, we had accepted the Poet's invitation. There we were, a community gathered together at twilight, sitting in an amphitheatre in silence, the colours of evening fading away as the night slowly rolled in. It was as if we had been entranced and left in the majestic embrace of nature. For how long we sat staring up at the 'starry night / That perfect economy', I cannot say.

The next thing any of us knew, someone toward the back started playing the oboe. It was a slow, distinctive melody, the kind that immediately pleases the ear, without being simplistic. The notes floated gracefully around the amphitheatre before lifting up to the heavens. We soon realised that the performance had not ended. After the first progression of the melody, a small group of violinists to my left stood up and joined in, complementing the oboe's melody with subtle harmonies. After the second progression, two flutists to my right joined this evolving performance, and all the musicians began moving toward the front, still playing their instruments. As they reached the front a band of trumpeters entered the fray, and on the next progression several cellists began playing loudly from the back, drawing the attention of the audience and offering depth and companionship to the music emanating from the front. By the time we had turned to face the front again, a choir of twenty had marched on stage, accompanied by a band of drummers who began to beat their instruments with zeal. Out of the corner of my eye I saw people begin lighting the torches that lined the tiers of the amphitheatre.

Then the choir began to sing, 'for all, for all, a poetic kiss', repeating this line over and over to the same enchanting melody that the oboe had introduced only minutes earlier. As the drums increased in volume and speed, the members of the choir inconspicuously morphed their lyrics into 'furor, furor, poeticus!', sending the drummers into a state of frenzy. The festivities were underway!

♦ ♦ ♦

Our community is just that – a community. We have time in our days to exchange a story with our neighbours, share our surpluses, and talk about what needs to be done. Perhaps someone needs to borrow one of the neighbourhood's saws; or needs assistance looking after the children; or needs advice on how to prune the grapevine; or needs tutelage in math or sculpture. Our way of life both promotes and requires the sharing of our resources, assets, and skills, and this promotes community. Furthermore, it turns out great fulfilment flows from taking part in community life, and from governing ourselves and our economy, even when the activities are not always glamorous. We have built a life that is interconnected and interdependent, and we are the better for it. We play hard together at work, and work hard together at play. Even in the era of extreme scarcity, just following the

Great Disruption, there was still a sense in which the suffering our community endured was tolerable on the grounds that we were struggling together, as one. Suffering, when there is meaning attached to it, is usually tolerable. As Nietzsche famously said, those people who have a 'why' to live can bear almost any 'how'. But meaningless suffering is the most dreadful thing imaginable.

In the end, the prosperity we enjoy on the Isle flows directly from the fact that we understand the meaning of economy; that is, we have embraced material sufficiency. There is no demon within urging us to get ahead, to climb the social ladder until all the life in us is consumed. Given that everyone has 'enough', there is no need for anyone to steal anything – indeed, there is not much to steal! – and because we have found fulfilment in our simpler ways of living, the idea of enacting violence upon another member of the community is incomprehensible. People at peace with themselves do not abuse or oppress others. Accordingly, crime is essentially unheard of on the Isle, as is the pain, fear, and anxiety it typically brings. A deeper fulfilment still flows from the peace of mind that comes from respecting the land base and biosphere upon which the entire community of life depends. Having our basic needs secured, and choosing not to dedicate our lives to the unlimited pursuit of more, we are left with the exhilarating and perhaps terrifying project of creating as an aesthetic project the meaning of our own lives. We are poets of our own lives, writing and living verse in free association, and by doing so our culture demonstrates that a 'simple life' can be a 'good life' – a truth that is obscured only to those who have not sufficiently explored their imaginations. This, in short, is our poetic conception of life.

The words of John Burroughs can hardly be improved on:

> *To be in direct and personal contact with the sources of your material life; to find the universal elements enough; to find the air and the water exhilarating; to be refreshed by a morning walk or an evening saunter; to find a quest of wild berries more satisfying than a gift of tropical fruit; to be thrilled by the stars at night; to be elated over a bird's nest or a wild flower in spring – these are some of the rewards of the simple life.*

Thus, in our simplicity, we are happy.

5

Politics and the Art of Freedom

With the economy and culture of the Isle outlined, the question of our political arrangements need be deferred no longer. This political story, if nothing else, is unique, owing to our unique circumstances, but perhaps there are lessons in our experience that speak more broadly to the human situation. In this chapter I will endeavour to convey the lessons we have learned, in the hope of answering some important questions about how our society functions and why it prospers. As will be seen, this inquiry entangles us in a range of issues, including education, human nature, power, and property, as well as perennial questions about the meaning and practice of freedom. While this inevitably demands a more philosophical approach in places, the relevant issues can best be understood by examining how they have unfolded in our lived experience. Accordingly, I intend not only to describe the nature of our political structures, but also provide some insight into how political life took form within those structures.

When Entropia was launched all those years ago, the first generation arrived on the Isle to discover that no political arrangements had been pre-established: no systems, no rules, and no regulations. Paradoxically, this lack of design was an essential ingredient in Entropia's design, casting us back into a political 'state of nature' and burdening us, for better or for worse, with the responsibility of building a world of our own making. We had pre-established infrastructure, of course, just no politics. This meant that our community was left to muddle through this first era of our story as best we could, learning the art of self-governance by way of practice, as if we were apprentices of freedom without a master to guide us.

Good governance is a subtle art. Human beings may be 'social' by nature, but we only become 'political' through practice and effort. This being so, when our community discovered that there were no preordained governors who were to take charge of things, people immediately realised how untrained they were in the practice of politics. That is, they realised how much of their political responsibility they had abdicated, in the Old World, to their so-called representatives. Without representatives to govern, our community was left to govern itself, come what may.

In the absence of appointed leaders there will always be some people who step into such roles and begin directing, while others will be more inclined to receive direction. It by no means follows, of course, that they who self-appoint themselves as leaders are more likely to be the wisest or most worthy. Rather too often the exact opposite is the case. Most leaders, in fact, have much to learn from their quietest supporters. Nevertheless, leaders who volunteer themselves at least get the ball rolling, so to speak, and every now and then they even set it off in the right direction. Fortunately, this was the case on the Isle. According to oral history, a small group formed in the first few days, aware that the political question had to be addressed and without delay, and they made the sensible decision to organise a gathering of the entire community. In this inaugural meeting, held in the town hall on the afternoon of Entropia's third day, our political conversation began. Various people took turns addressing the community, raising various issues that in time would need to be attended to, but within the first hour the discussion had become administrative, deferring the deeper political issues for when the more pressing issues had been addressed. People were asked to try to match their skills and labour to suitable tasks, and soon enough they were organising themselves into groups that would start work on the most urgent tasks: growing and distributing food; preparing meals; operating the mains water systems and other social services; and ensuring that the available housing was sensibly and fairly allocated. There was much to be done, so the main message from that first meeting was simply: 'get involved, you are needed'. Unsurprisingly, a similar message defined the town meetings that occurred during and after the Great Disruption.

As things turned out, this simple message – 'get involved, you are needed' – became the backbone of our political body. It is the ethos that defines us as citizens, and it is why we call our political arrangements a system of 'direct' or 'participatory' democracy, even though we do have some decision-making bodies that represent the broader community. Prior to the Great Disruption, I should note, our political system was not far removed from a standard 'representative' model of democracy, but since then our politics have evolved. Our new structures can be summarised as follows. We have two councils: one that is elected on the basis of expertise, wisdom, and integrity; the other being composed of a revolving selection of the community (much like jury duty in the Old World). The 'Advisory Council', as the elected group is known, is tasked with formulating social and economic policies that best serve the common good. This council has no power to enact those policies, however, meaning that it can never become an oppressive hierarchy. It can only recommend its policies to the 'People's Council' – being the other council – which alone has the authority to establish or abolish new rules and regulations. Should there ever be a dispute or uncertainty over the interpretation of a rule or regulation, the Advisory Council is consulted and asked to recommend the best interpretation to the People's Council, which again has ultimate authority on the matter. Both councils aspire to consensus decision-making, and often achieve as much, but in the absence of consensus, motions are passed according to a majority vote process. As well as formulating policies, the councils also take care of what little bureaucratic or administrative work is required on the Isle.

While not everyone can be expected to be an 'expert' in all matters of governance, we know that any of us might one day be called upon to serve on the People's Council, so there is an unstated expectation that we all keep reasonably informed about matters of social import. We do this, I should add, not because we *have* to, but because we *want* to. It is part of what citizenship means. After all, a person would have few grounds for complaint if they disapproved of the actions of a governing authority but neither played any part in community life nor was informed sufficiently about the issues. Being a citizen is not like being a child who has a right to be cared for; it is more like being a partner in a social enterprise, where everyone has a role to play; where everyone has something important to offer and therefore the responsibility to offer it.

The members of the People's Council revolve every three months (at the turn of every season) on the basis of a random ballot; the Advisory Council changes once a year, by way of elections. This system ensures that the wisest and most astute policy makers are in charge of formulating a vision that serves the common good, while keeping the power solely in the hands of the broader community. Although everyone on the Isle lives simply in a material sense, members of the Advisory Council are expected to take a vow of poverty while in office, abstaining from all but the bare necessities of life, in order to demonstrate publicly that their interests lie with the common good. It is interesting to think about what democracies in the Old World would have been like had all parliamentarians been expected to live lives of radical simplicity during their time in office. Certainly, it would have been hard to question the authenticity and commitment of a political party formed on that basis.

The types of rules that our councils enact concern such things as resource use and distribution, taxation, and investment in public infrastructure, as well as other regulatory or management issues when they arise. More will be said about the most fundamental and important of these rules later. For now, however, it must be emphasised simply that the real political work of the community is done more directly by the community itself. Each of the three neighbourhoods has monthly 'town meetings', chaired by someone in the Advisory Council, in which issues of public interest are discussed. When necessary, the councillor is asked to raise an issue with the Advisory Council, thus providing an intimate connection between our policy advisors and the most relevant issues of the immediate community. These town meetings also serve as opportunities to organise community 'working bees', which are generally the means by which socially important work is done. At first, invitations are sought for volunteers to attend the working bees, and generally this achieves sufficient numbers, but in the absence of sufficient volunteers, more direct requests are made to community members or groups. Given that these labours are shared more or less equally amongst the community, they are undertaken without the need for any enforcement, because people understand the social dynamics at play. That is, we recognise that one person's investment in the common good at one time will be repaid immediately or down the track by someone else's investment. Whether this system of ours is anarchist (meaning 'without rulers') or simply democratic *proper* is a semantic issue to which we give little attention.

The defining feature of our system of governance, then, is that everyone plays a part, whether that is through the formal channels of council participation, or the less formal paths of attending town meetings, or organising and contributing to working bees. This general statement knows few exceptions, and the exceptions that do exist can be accommodated easily. It turns out that people generally enjoy taking part in community life, such that it does not stretch the truth to say that political engagement, far from being a burden to us, is a source of real fulfilment. Furthermore, the distinction between the 'personal' and the 'political' has become a fuzzy one for us, insofar as we understand that most of our personal actions have political implications – especially our consumption habits – an insight lost on traditional liberals. Gone are the days of thinking that citizenship consists merely of voting once every few years and otherwise leaving political matters to the politicians. No democracy could function properly if those were the ethics of citizenship; at most those ethics would produce the façade of democracy, *a la* Empire.

♦ ♦ ♦

Before going any further I should probably address the issue of 'human nature', because the traditional objection to political systems such as ours was that they relied upon too optimistic a conception of humanity. This broad objection holds that anarchism, or participatory democracy – or whatever a system such as our might be labelled – may be nice in theory, and derived from quite beautiful assumptions, but that human beings simply are not that cooperative. It would follow that a coercive state is required to incentivise socially beneficial behaviour and deter antisocial behaviour. This objection assumes that human beings have an inbuilt tendency to be parasitic on their communities, not willing nurturers of them, but that is an assumption our way of life falsifies. Given that we desired an inclusive and participatory democracy, we chose to live it into existence.

There are three main ways to understand why 'human nature' is no obstacle to our politics, based on considerations of freedom, ethics, and power. First of all, with respect to freedom, there is no such thing as human nature, if human nature means that people are predetermined to act in certain ways. Human beings may indeed have impulses, and external circumstances beyond our control will always influence our decision-making processes, but to blame 'human nature' for human behaviour is to degrade what it means to be human – what it means to be free. In other words, there are both internal and external factors that incentivise people to act in this way or that, but ultimately we are free to accept or reject those influences. That is what freedom means. Even with a knife at our throats – or even under the influence of a selfish gene, or capitalist structures – we are free to accept such circumstances submissively or die struggling against them. How we respond to our impulses and circumstances is up to us, and this existential freedom is something for which we must each take responsibility. Consequently, the nature of humanity is what we choose it to be, not something determined in advance. It follows that human nature can be no obstacle to our politics, because human nature, as such, does not exist.

So what of human ethics? Is that not enough of an obstacle to ruin any participatory democracy? Someone might well accept that human beings will be what they make of themselves and nothing else, but still insist that the necessary cooperation at the heart of a participatory democracy could never be maintained, because no matter how free people might be, almost everyone tends to express that freedom by privileging self-interest over the common good. The objection is that people simply are not going to spend their time participating in community service when they could be doing something else that more directly advances their interests. This point certainly holds some intuitive weight, but it assumes that there is a conflict between self-interest and the common good, which again is falsified by our experience. We have discovered that the best way to advance one's self-interest is to be active in the running of one's own community. Indeed, it could be said that our community spirit is derived as much from the desire to be happy as the impulse to be good. That is, we serve the common good because it is in our 'enlightened' self-interest to do so. By way of contrast, when individuals historically sought to advance their self-interest through self-aggrandisement and without much care for the common good, they soon discovered that their communities crumbled and with it much chance of a flourishing society. In this sense, at least, individualism is ignorance.

This is not the end of the challenges, however. If community involvement is indeed a source of happiness, and therefore not a heavy ethical burden to meet, some people might still object that participatory democracies cannot be maintained because people generally do not seek happiness so much as they seek power. Again, there are some historical grounds for taking this rather dark objection seriously, and eminent philosophers, such as Friedrich Nietzsche, have argued that there is in fact a 'will to power' that governs not only the realm of human consciousness and behaviour, but all reality. If that is so, perhaps participatory democracies inevitably will be ruined by power struggles.

Responding to this objection requires a closer look at what the ambiguous term 'power' actually means, and by doing so perhaps we can also clear up a pertinent misunderstanding that has been pervasive in historical interpretations of Nietzsche's doctrine of the 'will to power'. Critics and commentators have typically suggested that figures like Napoleon and Alexander the Great exemplify the 'will to power' to which Nietzsche referred. On this interpretation, which is quite plausible, vast armies and material riches are what Nietzsche meant by power. There is an alternative interpretation, however, which can perhaps be explained best by way of a story about Diogenes the Cynic – the man who lived a life of voluntary poverty to show that a free and meaningful life could not be measured by conventional accounts of wealth. Legend has it that Alexander the Great – the richest and most influential man in the world at the time – approached Diogenes, inspired by the simplicity of his life, and offered to supply him with anything he needed, to which Diogenes responded by merely asking Alexander to stand out of his sunlight. Who, then, was the more 'powerful' of the two? Who was 'freer'? Was it Alexander, who had conquered the whole world and therefore was able to offer Diogenes anything he wanted? Or was it Diogenes, who was perfectly content already with what little he had, and so desired nothing that Alexander could provide? My point is that power is a concept that is relative to the goals which power is hoped to achieve, and in our community on the Isle, people understand Diogenes to be more powerful than Alexander. It follows that even if there is a 'will to power' that governs human consciousness, including in Entropia, it by no means follows that this is an obstacle to a flourishing participatory democracy. Indeed, it is the foundation of it, insofar as we are disciples of Diogenes. We do not seek to control armies and riches, but the circumstances of our own lives, and our power and freedom derive not from getting everything we want, but from wanting what we have – and being content with that.

To dedicate one's life to the attainment of power *external* to oneself is a confusion of desire, a confusion that defined the cultures of Empire. When reflecting back on those times, it is all too easy to see that the fetish for wealth, fame, and status, was really nothing more than a poorly orientated search for love, respect, and Diogenian power. If only people had walked a more direct path to what they ultimately desired, the world would have been a very different place. True power – the power we have in Entropia – resides peacefully within they who are in control of their own lives, not within they who control the lives of others.

♦ ♦ ♦

At this stage the role of education in our community should be addressed, for it is fair to say that sound education is what makes our way of life possible. I am not referring to the thorough training and guidance our children and young adults receive in the practical skills of life – especially gardening, sewing, energy conservation, and conflict resolution – important though those lessons are. Nor am I referring to the vast array of intellectual or artistic studies on offer at the Academy, which people undertake throughout their lives. I refer instead to the lessons we all receive in the 'philosophy of wealth', through which we engage questions about how to live a meaningful and fulfilling life in a world of limited resources. Of particular importance is the formal and informal education we receive in relation to money and material possessions, for ignorance on these matters insidiously brings ruin to one and all. Like any society, the ideas and values to which we are exposed inevitably become reflected in our lives, and this has enormous political implications. As such, education is a subject that deserves some elaboration.

It was the arch-poet Goethe who once wrote: 'All truly wise thoughts have been thought already thousands of times; but to make them truly ours, we must think them over again honestly, till they take root in personal experience'. This insight applies especially to the philosophy of wealth, for it is not enough merely to think wise thoughts about money and possessions; individuals must learn how to infuse those insights into lived experience. In attempting to achieve this we are assisted greatly by an edited anthology, called *Meditations on Simplicity*, which was first published on the Isle almost sixty years ago. It brings together some of the best writings on the philosophy of wealth, both ancient and contemporary, including contributions from the likes of Marcus Aurelius, John Ruskin, William Morris, Henry Thoreau, and Mahatma Gandhi. This resource is supplemented by many pages of thought experiments and practical exercises that help to illuminate and reinforce the book's essential insights. Still used widely today, the main themes of the book are summarised well in its opening paragraph:

> *As biophysical life forms, human beings obviously require a certain material standard of living to prosper, and below a certain threshold, we suffer. When people are hungry, they understandably desire more food; when people are cold, warmer clothing and adequate housing are critically important; when people are ill, they naturally want access to basic medical supplies. But when our basic needs for food, clothing, shelter, medical care, etc. are met, is more material wealth a goal for which we should constantly strive? How much is actually needed to live a full and prosperous life? And does there come a point when getting materially richer stops contributing to wellbeing? Ancient but ever new, these questions deserve sustained attention throughout our lives, for they expose the hidden pitfalls of greed and acquisitiveness, while illuminating the path of genuine prosperity. A society that neglects such questions does so at its own peril.*

I remember studying this text closely throughout my schooling years, and beyond the classroom its themes inevitably arise in all sorts of conversations and situations. This is not surprising, of course, given that the book addresses not merely the philosophy of wealth, but the philosophy of life itself. Even today I dip into its pages regularly, as a source of inspiration, guidance, and affirmation, and like most people, I have a copy lying around the house, the pages respectfully worn with many years of attention.

Before I unpack the political implications of our education with respect to wealth, let me briefly recount a recent experience of mine, which provides a little more insight into what issues our syllabus invites people to consider. Wandering home through the central garden one afternoon, I paused to admire our two small libraries – the bastions of our educational system – nestled within a circle of cedars. I reflected on how wonderful it was to have access to such extraordinary resources, how wonderful it was to have the greatest minds in history gathered together, waiting for us to engage them in silent conversation. We used to have three libraries, I should note, but tragically lost one in a fire shortly before the Great Disruption, and with it a significant period of historical and cultural knowledge. It is painful to think of what we lost in this blaze, but I suppose it reinforces the importance of thinking for ourselves and living in the present. Anyway, my attention was soon drawn away from the libraries and toward one of the open-aired rotundas behind me, where I heard one of my colleagues at the Academy, a psychologist, addressing a class of school students. As I moved nearer I noticed that the class was discussing themes raised in Henry David Thoreau's, *Walden*, so I decided to join the class quietly, drawn in by fond memories of my own schooling years. I took notes on the following conversation, in which a thoughtful student was challenging the professor:

> *Student:* It is not clear to me why material simplicity is the virtue you and Thoreau say it is. Is it not the case that money brings freedom and power? And is it not the case that with freedom and power we can live the life we have imagined?
>
> *Teacher:* These are good questions, but keep your mind open as we explore them more deeply. The relationship between material wealth and human wellbeing is complex and at times counter-intuitive. Human beings tend to think that getting richer will always improve their lives, on the assumption that they can use money in the marketplace to satisfy their most pressing desires, and up to a point, this may be true. In circumstances of material destitution, for example, getting richer is likely to improve a person's life. But just as the pursuit of material wealth can bring benefits, it also exacts costs – such as time and ecological impact – and it turns out that there comes a point when the costs begin to outweigh the benefits. Beyond that point, the pursuit of wealth becomes, you might say, 'uneconomic' or wasteful. Indeed, beyond a surprisingly low threshold, getting richer in material terms stops contributing significantly to wellbeing. This conclusion is supported both by ancient wisdom traditions and by modern empirical studies, even if our intuitions or instincts sometimes lead us to assume otherwise. You will find that throughout history people have sought happiness by accumulating money and possessions, only to discover that happiness resides elsewhere.

Student: But why is it, exactly, that material wealth does not lead to happiness? Respectfully, I remain sceptical. After all, if someone walked up to you this very moment and gave you a bag of gold, would that not make you happy?

Teacher: I am happy to say that I am already happy, so why should I want to lug around a heavy bag of gold? In any case, people don't just walk up to us and give us gold, we have to work for it, and personally, I would rather do other things with my time than work for superfluous wealth. But seriously, the issue is about finding the right balance. Let us examine this issue from the perspective of human psychology. Gold, jewels, fine clothing, sparkling ornaments, splendid houses, dazzling technologies, and so forth, may seem glamorous, but such things tend to provide only fleeting satisfaction, at most, eventually leaving people feeling unsatisfied, and forever wanting something more. Evidence suggests that human beings simply do not find superfluous consumption all that fulfilling, despite what the advertisements in the Old World used to promise. On the other hand, deeper and more enduring fulfilment does seem to flow from many non-materialistic sources of wellbeing, such as social engagement, creative activity, spiritual exploration, and time to enjoy the wonders of the natural world – none of which relies on money, or much money. What this means is that people can live very humble yet fulfilling lives, provided basic material needs are met. Affluence is by no means a precondition for human flourishing, and it can even be a social poison.

Student: If that is so, why did previous cultures dedicate so much of their energies to the pursuit of material wealth? Why didn't they realise that affluence was not the path to prosperity? Sometimes I wonder whether we might enjoy a consumer way of life more than the simplicity of life on the Isle.

Teacher: It is natural to wonder about such things, but before you pursue affluence, bear this in mind: one of the problems with a consumer-orientated way of life is that people adapt to their material circumstances, and having adapted, their material expectations rise, leaving people constantly dissatisfied no matter how rich they might become. This phenomenon typically escapes notice, however, because its effects emerge slowly. At first the tepee was a happy advance on the cave, but then humans adapted to the tepee and wanted a hut; then they adapted to the hut and wanted a house; then a nicer house; then a bigger house; then a mansion, and so forth. But they who acquired a mansion inevitably became accustomed, even to such luxurious surroundings, and found themselves dissatisfied still, so they would seek a castle; then two castles; then all the castles. As people climb this ladder, they also tend to desire more luxurious and exotic foods, finer clothing, and more expensive jewels, to match the splendour of their castle.

Student: Are you saying that there is no final rung on the ladder of material desire, no end to the rat race?

Teacher: Precisely. My point is that if left to themselves, material desires will consume a human being until the moment of death, at which point it is too late to realise that the best things in life are free. Material desires need to be controlled, they need to be disciplined, or else they will lead us astray. Too many people have misspent their lives in the pursuit of things that were incapable of bringing lasting happiness. Too many have lain on their deathbeds amongst their fabulous riches, suffering the terrible pain of regret. But, please, do not take my word for any of this. As always, you must think for yourselves.

Student: I certainly do not want to die only to discover that I had not really lived – that much is clear to me!

Teacher: I am glad to hear this, but take note: even if you come to accept these lessons *in theory*, they can be very challenging to *practise*. How easy it is to lament the shallow endeavours of the materialist only then to spend all one's time working to fund the very same lifestyle! Historically, many people were guilty of living this glaring contradiction.

Student: How, then, do we avoid this contradiction?

Teacher: The only reliable way to avoid the pitfalls of materialism and acquisitiveness is to practise what can be called 'mindful sufficiency'. This practice lies at the centre of our lessons in the philosophy of wealth, and in a sense we are practising it right now. Put simply, mindful sufficiency calls on us to meditate regularly on the question 'how much is enough?' Only by taking this question seriously can we arrive at the marvellous realisation that 'just enough is plenty'. Of course, far from being a new teaching, this is simply a dedicated application of ancient Stoic wisdom.

Student: What did the Stoics have to say about all this? Could you elaborate?

Teacher: I would be happy to. The Stoics argued that, while people cannot always be in control of how much worldly wealth and fame they attain, they are or can be in control of the attitudes they adopt in relation to such things. Accordingly, if a person lets their material desires escalate without limit, it may be that the person remains dissatisfied even in conditions of extreme opulence. But if someone thinks seriously about how much is actually needed to live a meaningful and happy life, they might find that they already have all they need, and so do not need to waste any more time and energy on materialistic pursuits.

Student: I suppose this means that two people both living lives of radical simplicity might experience such a low-consumption way of life in totally different ways, depending on the mindset that they bring to experience.

Teacher: You are right, again. Where one person bemoans how little they have, the other celebrates and affirms life because they have so much! Fortunately, the mindset is in our control, even if the circumstances may not always be. The path of mindful sufficiency, however, takes practice and discipline, for one must constantly be on guard against the seductions of wealth, fame, and status. But the journey is a rewarding one, so let us keep to the path.

♦ ♦ ♦

I reproduce this conversation merely as an example of the types of inquiry that our system of education encourages. We encourage these inquires, I should emphasise, because the relationship between material wealth and wellbeing is not always obvious, *thus requiring education*. We cannot assume that people will naturally understand this surprisingly complex subject without guidance. Indeed, human beings consistently tend to overestimate the value of money and possessions, and underestimate the value of non-materialistic sources of wellbeing. But this calculus is far too important to get wrong. Accordingly, we feel it is of the utmost importance that the philosophy of wealth is built into our educational teachings, from childhood onwards, because the implications of misunderstanding these issues are socially and ecologically disastrous, as Empire discovered. By way of contrast, we educate ourselves into a life of material simplicity, and therein we find the good life.

Sound education in relation to material wealth, however, is not just important from a personal and social perspective. My reason for addressing these issues in this chapter is because the philosophy of wealth also has profound political implications. Human beings only have a limited amount of time and energy with which to live their lives. It follows that the more time and energy a society dedicates to the pursuit of material wealth, the less it will have for other things, such as community or political engagement. Taken to its extreme, such a society may end up extremely affluent, but comprising individuals who are alienated, disengaged, and lonely – and so not rich at all. Similarly, the more important affluence is to individuals or societies, the less willing they will be to share wealth for reasons of social justice, and the less willing they will be to voluntarily limit consumption for the sake of environmental health. It follows that a just and sustainable society cannot be a society dedicated to the never-ending pursuit of affluence, but must instead be based on material sufficiency. This has political implications because, as Aristotle once wrote, 'a person who is going to make a fruitful inquiry into the best political arrangement, must first set out clearly what the most choiceworthy life is. For if that is unclear, the best political arrangement must also be unclear'.

Having put forward the 'simple life' as the most choiceworthy life, the remainder of this chapter will outline some of the key features of our politics of sufficiency.

♦ ♦ ♦

During the Great Disruption our community faced some very hard questions about how we were to live. In particular, we had to make democratic decisions about how we were going to structure our economy, how we were going to govern social relations, and what values were to shape and define these efforts. It was decided that we should work toward creating a constitutional document that would state, in the clearest terms possible, the kind of society we wanted to live in. This document was not intended to end our political debates, but to provide a starting point, a framework within which we could debate and move forward. In the first meeting to discuss this matter there was immediate and unanimous agreement that we all wanted a society that was free, just, and sustainable, but it took almost a year of further meetings to unpack those noble but vague sentiments in written form. Eventually a short constitutional document was drafted by the Advisory Council and put to a referendum by the People's Council, and this document received 94 per cent support. It is reproduced in its entirety below, as it serves as the best summary of our social, economic and political vision.

Charter of the Deep Future

ENOUGH, FOR EVERYONE, FOREVER

We affirm that providing 'enough, for everyone, forever' is the defining objective of our economy, which we seek to achieve by working together in free association.

We affirm that everyone is free to create as an aesthetic project the meaning of their own lives, while acknowledging that this freedom legitimately extends only so far as others can have the same freedom. Freedom thus implies restraint.

We affirm that our inclusive democracy does not discriminate on such grounds as race, ethnicity, gender, age, sexuality, politics, or faith.

We affirm that generations into the deep future are entitled to the same freedoms as present generations.

We affirm that respecting the deep future requires maintaining a healthy environment.

We affirm that technology can help to protect our environment only if it is governed by an ethics of sufficiency, not an ethics of growth. Efficiency without sufficiency is lost.

We affirm that maintaining a healthy environment requires creating a stationary state economy that operates within environmental and energy limits.

We affirm that a stationary state means stabilising consumption and population, transitioning to renewable sources of energy, and adapting to reduced energy supply.

We affirm that strict limits on material accumulation are required if a stationary state is to maintain a just distribution of resources and avoid corrosive inequalities.

We affirm that property rights are justifiable only to the extent they serve the common good, including the overriding interests of humanitarian and ecological justice.

We affirm that a stationary state economy depends on a culture that embraces lifestyles of material sufficiency and rejects lifestyles of material affluence.

We affirm that material sufficiency in a free society provides the conditions for an infinite variety of meaningful, happy, and fulfilling lives.

'The Charter', as it is referred to, obviously leaves open many questions of detail, but as stated above, it is sufficiently suggestive of a way of life to provide us with a useful starting point. This is not the place to work laboriously through the various rules and regulations that we have created in interpretation of the Charter, but a few words should be offered in elaboration.

Our stationary state economy did not emerge spontaneously. It was a project that required effort and commitment. We began by trying to establish how much land was required to provide everyone on the Isle with their most basic material and energy needs, such as food, clothing, shelter, and heat for warmth and cooking. We then tried to assess how much more land and energy was required to provide our community with those things beyond a basic subsistence – tools of various sorts – that could help us flourish in modest comfort. I am referring here to things like spades, saws, axes, hammers, cooking utensils, matches, bicycles, carts, trains, paper, books, glass, musical instruments, medicines and basic medical equipment, and a significant list of other basic or more technical tools. This complex exercise in economic and ecological accounting gave us a sense of how much land and energy were needed to provide 'enough, for everyone, forever', and it provided us with guidance about where we should set the boundary of our stationary state economy. We felt that in order to live within ecological and energy limits we needed to know how much we had legitimately available to us, and we have become highly skilled in measuring with precision the extent of our economic activities and their (limited) ecological impacts. By strictly regulating the overall scale of our economic activities, we are able to maintain a mildly fluctuating stationary state economy. The use and distribution of resources are in constant flux, of course, but in terms of overall biophysical demand, the economy has more or less attained a state of dynamic equilibrium. But as John Stuart Mill (the originator of the stationary state concept) insisted, a stationary state economy does not imply any stationary state in human improvement.

Given that we have voluntarily stabilised production and consumption flows through our economy, the issue of distributive justice necessarily took a new form. In the Old World, distributive justice was understood widely to mean the outcome of free market transactions, and if free markets left some people in poverty, then economic growth was the means by which it was assumed everyone could be lifted out of poverty. In other words, achieving distributive justice in the Old World was about growing the economic pie, not slicing it differently. Given that our stationary state economy does not grow, however, it follows that questions of distributive justice must be solved more directly, by ensuring that everyone has a fair share of what we have. This requires two main distributive mechanisms: The Basic Income and the Maximum Wage.

The core idea of the Basic Income is relatively straightforward. Every individual on the Isle receives a fortnightly credit of vouchers, and these vouchers are sufficient for an individual to live at a minimal though dignified standard of economic security. The vouchers can be redeemed (if necessary) at the town hall on any day of the week, where food, clothing, medical attention, and other basic needs are available. Paid for through taxation and donation, this Basic Income is *guaranteed* by the People's Council, *unconditional* on the performance of any labour, and *universal*. Parents are the custodians of their children's credits. If a person or family does not have access to decent shelter or arable land, they are entitled to live in publically funded accommodation until a small plot of land is allocated to them and a community building project is organised. This policy defines our politics of sufficiency by socialising the provision of basic material needs.

Within our Basic Income system, other welfare transfers are unnecessary – such as unemployment benefits, family allowances, pensions – since the Basic Income entitlement is sufficient to provide everyone with a decent, though minimal, subsistence. Poverty, whether from incapacity or unemployment, is therefore eliminated. Our Basic Income system does not defer the responsibility of helping the poor to some future occasion or treat poverty as a 'regrettable necessity'; nor does it require a large administrative bureaucracy. Instead, it is a policy based on the idea that the distribution of an economy's wealth must begin by ensuring that everyone has 'enough' to live with dignity. Not until that basic condition is met can the economy's wealth be distributed further.

Historically, the feasibility of a Basic Income System was questioned on two main grounds. The first objection was that making the Basic Income unconditional on the performance of any labour would give rise to a society of 'free-loaders' and ultimately lead to economic collapse. This objection, however, arises out of a false conception of human beings. While it may be the case that the 'free-loader' problem exists to some minimal extent on the Isle, our society shows that human beings, by and large, are social creatures, who find being engaged in their community's work more meaningful and fulfilling than being isolated, idle, and parasitic on their community. Furthermore, even the small minority that does not always pull its own weight proves to be a tolerable social burden – more tolerable, we believe, than the existence of poverty.

The second objection historically levelled at the Basic Income concerned its financial feasibility. This is a pragmatic issue that is obviously of great importance, although it turned out to be more a matter of political commitment than a financing challenge, especially given how simply we all live anyway. To ease the financial burden and soften the transition, our policy approach was to begin with a Negative Income Tax system, which differs from a Basic Income in that it provides voucher-credits, not universally, but only to those with incomes below the subsistence level. This provided low-income earners or the unemployed with a guaranteed minimum income but via an alternative route. Over time the Negative Income Tax System evolved into a Basic Income System, although in practice these policies were very similar.

The social benefits of a successful Basic Income System are profound and far-reaching. Beyond eliminating poverty and economic insecurity, its institution also strengthens the bargaining position of workers, since it gives people a property right that is independent of their paid employment, and thus more power to demand decent working conditions. It also means that people do not have to accept alienating, exploitative, or degrading jobs just to survive; nor is there any pressure to sacrifice social and political autonomy in order to achieve economic security. Furthermore, a Basic Income also acknowledges the worth of unpaid caring work and other forms of social contribution, thereby extending economic citizenship beyond participants in the traditional labour market or 'formal economy'. For these reasons, among others, our Basic Income System has produced a far more democratic and egalitarian society than any capitalist society ever could.

As well as a Basic Income – or income 'floor' – our stationary state economy also maintains an income 'ceiling' – that is, an upper limit to the size of any individual's income. We call this policy the Maximum Wage, and it is achieved through our tax system. Our tax rate increases progressively as the taxable income increases, culminating in a 100 per cent tax on all income over a specified level (currently situated at approximately four times the value of the Basic Income). This policy is based on the understanding that great inequalities of wealth are socially and politically corrosive. It finds further justification on the grounds that once basic material needs are met, further increases in income contribute little if anything to human wellbeing. This means a Maximum Wage is an extremely important means of avoiding wasteful consumption and creating a more egalitarian society. The tax procured from the Maximum Wage is used to fund the Basic Income and other community initiatives. I should also note that we have abolished all laws of inheritance and bequest, which provides another means of ensuring that wealth remains broadly distributed on the Isle. Upon death, a person's property becomes the property of the community, and is distributed by the People's Council according to the principle of 'most pressing need'. As a secondary principle, the council will also take into consideration whether an asset or item is of particular sentimental value to a family, and distribute it accordingly.

All this means we have a rather unique property and tax system. While we have not abolished private property, as such, the councils govern much of our land and all our essential services (water, electricity, transport, etc.); and our Basic Income ensures that everyone has a stake in the community's economic output. Even property rights that are deemed 'private' necessarily have social responsibilities attached them, given that we consider ourselves 'stewards' of the land, who hold it in trust for the future. We recognise that private property is a concept that can take any number of institutional forms, and this means that it is up to our community to define and limit the contours of property rights, because property rights are not self-defining. The nature of our property system, therefore, depends mainly on the social values that give property rights their institutional content, and this means that private property rights can be legitimately constrained if they clash with the common good.

♦ ♦ ♦

The political question of population control is another clear example of how, paradoxically, we restricted freedom to maximise freedom; that is, how we restricted some life choices of the current generation so that future generations could flourish, as we were flourishing, in a healthy environment. We realised that population growth on a finite land base represented a trend that was unsustainable, for the obvious reason that all human beings depend on nature for their sustenance – for food to eat, clothes to wear, shelter to keep us warm, energy and tools to use, and so forth. It follows that the more people there are, the greater the burden on nature (all other things being equal). Even a simple living culture such as our own would eventually overwhelm its land base, with catastrophic consequences, if population kept growing endlessly into the future. Population growth, therefore, is inevitably a question that every society must face at some time or other, or suffer the consequences of eco-systemic collapse.

The problem is that procreation seems like such a personal and intimate process, and in a sense it obviously is. That was why traditional liberals felt that this was a subject that should not be regulated by any governing authority. But obviously the so-called 'private' nature of procreation becomes much less private when it has enormous, potentially life-threatening, ecological consequences. It is very easy to understand why future generations would be aggrieved if they were left a degraded environment due to the reluctance of earlier generations to regulate population. The freedoms of history can evolve into the chains of the future, and it only takes a small imaginative effort to realise that this is so with respect to population and consumption. Accordingly, to ensure the liberties of the future, we were required to constrain the liberties of the present. Intellectually there is nothing controversial about this, but emotionally it gave rise to a firestorm. It thus took courage for us to face this issue, but today our approach has entered commonsense. It was an issue, I suppose, much like the historic abolishment of slavery or segregation – what one generation considered unthinkable, the next generation could not imagine being otherwise. Such is the way with great moral advances.

When debating the question of how, exactly, we were to deal with the issue of population growth, people came up with all sorts of clever ways to try to achieve a sustainable population without direct regulation – incentivising this, disincentivising that. But ultimately it became clear that this was just being evasive, or, as one critic put it more bluntly: 'such proposals are just fudging the issue'. In the end it was decided that if a sustainable population was what we desired and indeed required, there would simply have to be rules governing how many children people could have. As I said, this approach proved extremely controversial. Many people felt that it was too early to consider such regulations. Others felt that a sustainable population should be achieved by choice, rather than decree. But when people came to consider the issue with their minds rather than their hearts, it was hard to avoid the conclusion that deferring the question of population was rather like passing the buck, which would have been a cowardly dereliction of duty. Accordingly, after weeks of often heated debate, the Advisory Council submitted a policy proposal to the People's Council, which eventually was passed and used as the basis of a referendum. The policy, outlined below, received 68 per cent support at the time, but over the years that support has grown considerably, and today there is little disagreement over the essence of the policy.

The policy, which is remarkably simple, states that the Isle must 'ensure population stays within sustainable bounds', and over the three generations since the Great Disruption we have been successful at meeting this goal. At the end of every year, our population is counted and our land base is assessed, and that information allows us to ascertain how many Certificates of Procreation can be awarded upon application. Our policy holds that every individual has a right to be biologically connected to one child, without the need for a certificate, but to have further children people must apply. In determining who is awarded certificates, applicants with fewer children are always privileged over those with more, and if there is nothing distinguishing various applicants, then the available certificates are awarded randomly within that subset.

As simple and effective as this policy is, there are, of course, complications. First of all, there is nothing that can be done about accidental or unplanned pregnancies, for we are certainly not going to remove a child from its parents, and it would be abhorrent to enforce terminations under any circumstances. So we have to accept unplanned pregnancies as inevitable, and simply educate ourselves well and make contraception easily available. This minimises the chances of unplanned pregnancies and it turns out this has not proven to be a significant problem. Another complexity arises when relationships that have produced children dissolve and new relationships are developed. Are such relationships entitled to a child if either or both of the members have had a child already? Our policy is to treat such relationships as a blank slate – entitling them to at least one child – but we then take previous children into account should applications be made for further children. The most challenging issue, however, is what happens should someone deliberately flout the policy (or falsely claim a pregnancy was unplanned). Again, as a moral issue, we know the child cannot be removed from the parents, nor do we think it suitable to impose penalties of any sort. So ultimately our policy is not enforced, as such. How can it be? All we can do is publish the policy as a democratically endorsed rule, clearly explain its rationale, and trust that a culture arises that respects it. So far this policy has been sufficient to keep our population within sustainable bounds, even allowing for those individuals who ignore it. Fortunately, because our culture shares many of the responsibilities of raising children, people who choose not to have children of their own still have many opportunities to be around children and be enriched by their wonder.

The most unsettling consequence of our population policy, however, is the social stigma that attaches to those who flout the policy. Given the firm moral basis of our policy, there inevitably arises a sense that those who flout the policy have done 'something wrong', even if they do not happen to agree with the policy. But this stigma, regrettable though it is, is a burden we are required to bear for the greater good that our policy serves. If anyone had expected there to be a painless 'solution' to the problem of population growth they were rather expecting too much.

♦ ♦ ♦

In closing this chapter I should make clear that however much common ground we share in Entropia, there nevertheless remains – and should remain! – many areas where people fervently disagree. We may all walk in solidarity under the banner of 'enough, for everyone, forever', but that hardly means we are a homogenous polity that agrees on all matters of detail. For example, there are ongoing debates over how best to use or distribute resources, which public infrastructure projects are most pressing, what levels of taxation are most suitable, or how far into the wild our economy should reach. One would only need to attend a single town meeting in Entropia to see that we are far from being of single mind! While our debates retain a certain civility – most of the time, at least – that does not imply an absence of emotion or conviction. Indeed, there remain matters not just of detail but of real substance about which people vehemently disagree and may continue to disagree, including the recent debate about whether we should be killing animals for food. A society in which there was no disagreement or conflict would not be a human society – and even if such a society were to arise, chances are it would be terribly dull.

Politics, therefore, could be described as the art of living well with people who disagree with you. The fact is, intelligent and reasonable people can and do disagree, and political maturity involves negotiating these debates respectfully and earnestly, whether in a town meeting or around a dinner table. This requires practice and training, as well as patience and creativity. Arguments must be presented clearly and with reference to evidence, but sometimes the issue of assessing the balance of conflicting evidence is one that offers no clear answer, or is capable of various reasonable interpretations. In such times it is important that different sides of the debate make genuine efforts to assess the issue from different perspectives, knowing that there is more than one way to look at the world. If agreement remains elusive, participants in political debate must then make decisions about whether a compromise or further compromise should be made, whether a more imaginative solution can be formed, or whether the various parties must remain at the negotiating table in the hope that further discourse will produce a mutually acceptable path forward. None of this ensures political harmony, but these basic methods provide the most likely path to peace and prosperity, provided they are applied with humility, sincerity, and imagination.

Thus, in our simplicity, we are free.

6

Awakening of Spirit

The subject of this chapter seems to call for a more personal narrative, so forgive me for using a humble journey of my own as medium through which to engage themes of infinitely greater significance. The story begins not so long ago, on an evening when I felt the sudden and compelling need for solitude. For reasons that were unclear to me, I had lost composure and balance in life, and I wanted to get away from all of life's distractions in the hope of gaining some new perspective. So I packed a rucksack and set out for the mount, to where I would often journey in times of personal unrest.

This was the kind of freedom we had on the Isle. Whenever someone needed space and solitude, one only needed to walk away, into the wild, whenever and for however long one desired. It was an immense spiritual privilege, one that I understand distinguishes us from most of civilised humankind that went before us. There was not even an obligation to tell anyone, although in this instance I left a note on my door stating simply that I had gone for a long walk and that I would return 'when the wind blew me back'. My peers would understand.

Wisdom traditions seem to agree that composure in life demands the regular therapy of solitude – sufficient time to delve into one's own depths, and sufficient space to craft a calm, mindful, and deliberate approach to life, beyond the gaze and expectations of society. Without such time and space, one tends to get caught up in the unfreedom of the world's currents and thrown about this way and that, like a rag doll; and if it is not the world's currents placing obstacles in life's path, then it is one's own undisciplined emotions and desires. It is my understanding that in the frantic, urban lifestyles of industrial civilisation, moments of peace and tranquillity in the midst of nature did not come easily. It is no wonder, then, that history books refer to a 'spiritual malaise' that permeated the West, and that old poets spoke of angst and misery as being 'the rivers of the world'. Fortunately, our rivers on the Isle flowed to a very different rhythm, even if rocks and fallen trees still upset that rhythm at times, as I had discovered.

It was a clear night in early autumn. As a bright, full moon hung low in the sky, I headed east through the woods, using the Southern Cross as my compass. My motives were as unclear as the air was crisp and fresh. All I knew was that I wanted distance, space, and solitude, and as the creatures of the night came out to greet me, I discovered that my wishes had been granted.

I stopped to fill my flask at the river. As I gazed at the shimmering reflection of the moon on the water, I thought I saw the pale green eyes of a small animal flicker on the far shore. By the time I looked up, however, the animal had moved on, or disappeared into the night's shadows. My attention was soon drawn to the *whooo whoooo* of a laughing owl, which seemed to be calling me eastward. I took a sip of water and continued on my way.

It is a mysterious pleasure how nourishing a solitary walk in the woods can be. One is alone but never lonely. I take special delight when all directions look the same, for this gives the impression that space has imploded into a simpler dimension, where not even time complicates things. As I sauntered deeper into the woods I found myself stepping more lightly, as if I were in the process of shedding the burden of my vague worries and concerns, leaving them behind as existential waste, as compost, to rejuvenate the earth that was rejuvenating me.

Already the first of my troubles had become clear. For the last six weeks I had been so absorbed in finishing my new literary composition, working intensively on it day and night, that I had forgotten to go outside very often, not even to the garden. Hunched over my desk, back sore, passionately scribbling away in a frenzy, I had been in a world of my own – a stimulating one, to be sure, but one that I now see was dangerously disconnected from the natural world and lacking balance. As I breathed the autumn air that night I found myself being reminded of how distant I had been from the cosmos. At the same time, my long absence from nature had made my return to the woods all the more intoxicating. It was as if nature were punishing me with kindness for the neglect I had shown. 'Look what you have been missing, careless child!' Mother Earth seemed to be saying, confident that her sublime spell had been successfully cast upon me. I was indeed a willing object of her magic and a reborn subject of her majesty. I drank from the evening deeply, my senses alight with gratitude and appreciation.

I found myself speaking Emerson's words out loud, offering them unto the wild, like a prayer:

> *In good health, the air is a cordial of incredible virtue. Crossing a bare common, in snow puddles, at twilight, under a clouded sky, without having in my thoughts any occurrence of special good fortune, I have enjoyed a perfect exhilaration. I am glad to the point of fear.*

The scene I was crossing that night might have been different from Emerson's, but his experience was one to which any nature mystic could relate. For a moment, however, rather than losing myself in nature's beauty, I was overcome, to my surprise, with an immense sadness. I began thinking of my ancestors in the industrial age who would work long hours, cramped up in offices or factories under artificial lights, and who would too often spend their evening hours in front of a television, hiding from the stars, seeking not so much entertainment as distraction. In those times, people's exposure to the outdoors must have been too often limited to walking through a concrete jungle to their car. Where was their rage for nature?

I fantasised that occasionally those urbanites would have noticed a weed reaching upward through a crack in the pavement and have been quietly reminded that concrete was not the whole world; that there was something terrifyingly beautiful that lay deeper; that nature, with love and forgiveness, was trying to reach out to human beings through the cracks of Empire, in spite of how badly she had been treated. I suspected it was more likely, however, that Empire would have already doused the weeds in chemicals in order to maintain the chic, urban or suburban aesthetic, hoping that nature would not intrude upon the grim tidiness of civilised life.

It is said that an old philosopher once gazed into the eyes of civilised man and claimed to see only faces 'twisted with despair'. Perhaps that explains why Empire took the suicidal form it did; why Empire subconsciously wished for its own demise, even as it seemed to struggle so vehemently for its continuance. My studies of history suggest to me strongly that those were indeed times of tragic deprivation, times when entire cultures were disconnected from the natural world upon which physical, mental and even spiritual health depends. If only people had been permitted time to isolate themselves from their industrial existence for long enough to unlearn it, for long enough to rouse themselves from the daze of unexamined habit and reopen the doors of perception –

perhaps that would have provoked a fresh and revolutionary interpretation of life. But, as it happened, children who were raised without any intimate connection with nature never knew what had been lost to the modern world, and therefore rarely sought to reignite such intimacy. Thinking of all this, as I walked through the magnificent woods, made me sad to the point of tears.

◆ ◆ ◆

There is something primordial about how exposure to nature helps to foster holistic health and how disconnection induces stress and anxiety. This must have been built into our very being over millions of years of evolutionary development. Humans are creatures of the elements, and we need to see the stars and feel the wind like we need oxygen. Take away the stars or blind us from the changing seasons, and insidiously the light of our being fades. The indigenous peoples of the world were tuned in to this relationship, but it was a truth lost to the more 'advanced' cultures, as it had been temporarily lost to me.

Although I had foolishly cut myself off from nature over recent weeks, I was warmed by the knowledge that our community on the Isle took being-in-nature seriously. Our way of life reflects the insight that being regularly outdoors, in close contact with the elements, is a necessary condition for a life of balance and inner peace. We make deliberate efforts to infuse 'the wild' into our everyday lives, knowing that these efforts are generously, if sometimes inconspicuously, repaid. Children and adults alike are always encouraged to take leisure outdoors, and many of the lessons at school or the Academy take place under an oak tree or in one of the open-aired rotundas in the central garden. Whenever practicable, the productive cooperatives follow suit. It is not uncommon to see artisans engaged in creative activity out in the fields, working peacefully in makeshift studios or workshops. Furthermore, groups of friends and families often journey around the Isle's various terrains on extended camping exhibitions, carrying everything they need for a dignified subsistence on their backs, as a reminder that Mother Earth provides for us in perfect abundance. More generally, the fact that we are all gardeners on the Isle generally keeps us intimately in touch with the seasons, the soil, and our souls. Gardening thus provides us with regular opportunities for active meditation; that is, opportunities to tend to ourselves as we tend to our crops.

I had been neglecting both spiritual practices in recent weeks – both soil and soul – and was the worse for it. Nevertheless, as I made my way toward the foot of the mount, while the moon rose slowly in the sky, I found myself being discreetly redeemed.

♦ ♦ ♦

As I reflected upon the existential implications of my own relationship with nature, my thoughts returned to the Old World. I came to see that the disconnection from nature in the age of Empire had consequences that ran deeper even than spiritual impoverishment. This disconnect unsurprisingly had personal effects, as people were denied the therapeutic medicine of time in the wild, and people suffered accordingly. Oh what a few months in the woods would have done for the subjects of Empire! But it was also the case that through their disconnection from nature, most people were unable to fall in love with nature, for the simple reason that one cannot easily fall in love with what one does not know. Today it is generally accepted that this inability to love Mother Earth, through lack of exposure to her, must have been why cultures in the Old World were so apathetic in the face of ecological degradation, and why nations and individuals alike were happy to box up the natural world as a mere commodity and sell it to the highest bidder. It suggests that Empire's ecological crisis was first and foremost a spiritual crisis – a crisis of cosmology and vision. It was a failure to see that all life is interconnected, and that violence against the oceans, the forests, and the skies – however distant that violence might seem – is akin to self-harm. For better or for worse, it took a Great Disruption to awaken us from this deep, masochistic slumber.

◆ ◆ ◆

After walking for many hours into the night, lost in reverie but physically on track, I came to a familiar clearing in the woods, near the foot of the mount. The absence of trees meant that light from the moon and stars was able to coat the picturesque scene with a heavenly silver gloss. This roughly oval clearing had a small creek running through it, and I took this opportunity to fill up my flask again and take a moment's rest. I lay down on a large fallen tree that was covered in soft, green moss and gazed up at the starry expanse. The night's abundant wildlife went about its business as if I were not there, and I returned to it this same courtesy.

Surveying the universe from my humble observatory, as much a part of nature as the moss upon which I lay, I breathed deeply and began thinking about how easy it is to lose composure and perspective in life; how easy it is to get caught up in trivialities and distracted by superfluities. I found it difficult to imagine how distracting life must have been in the consumer cultures of the Old World, when it appears materialistic cravings, encouraged by omnipresent advertisements, would constantly interfere with, and eternally defer, one's most meaningful pursuits. And to interfere with 'meaning' is a spiritual issue of the highest order, for it is the spirit that suffers most when it loses touch with meaning.

What is spiritual practice if not the humble and creative engagement of self, other, and nature, as sources of meaning? What is spiritual impoverishment if not giving up one's nourishing dreams and mysteries in exchange for 'nice things'?

My memory served me up an old parable written by the Danish philosopher, Soren Kierkegaard, which poetically addressed the spiritual dangers of materialism:

> *When prosperous people on dark but star-lit nights drive comfortably in their carriages and have the lanterns lighted, aye, then they are safe, they fear no difficulty, they carry their light with them, and it is not dark close around them. But precisely because they have the lanterns lighted, and have a strong light close to them, precisely for this reason they cannot see the stars, which the humble peasants driving without lights can see gloriously in the dark but starry night. So those deceived ones live in the temporal existence: either, occupied with the necessaries of life, they are too busy to avail themselves of the view, or in their prosperity and good days they have, as it were, lanterns lighted, and close about them everything is so satisfactory, so pleasant, so comfortable – but the view is lacking, the prospect, the view of the stars.*

Kierkegaard was offering a warning here that if people let material desires burn too brightly, they might find that it is harder to see the stars; by which he meant, of course, harder for people to enjoy the benefits of spiritual experience. Conversely, those who are less concerned about accumulating material wealth, and who are prepared to live more simply and humbly, are likely to find the spiritual path less cluttered, allowing for a clearer view of the stars. This message is ancient but of universal concern, even if it is also a message that must be interpreted through one's own, individual lens of understanding. Spiritual practice is certainly a 'private' matter, not because it must be done alone, but because no one can do it for us.

In the dark but star-lit times of Empire, Kierkegaard's timeless parable deserved much more attention than it received, especially in that era immediately preceding the Great Disruption, when the materialism of consumer culture was burning more brightly than ever, obscuring the view of the stars. Industrial civilisation was a world of mass-produced commodities, but in such a world, what room was there for an original relation to the universe? Science, apparently, had solved all the mysteries of human existence, or at least had the method to solve them – making metaphysics unnecessary and wonder seem childlike or naïve. Once the heart of human civilisation, spiritual perspectives had become culturally taboo, and were treated only condescendingly by mass media, if at all. Politicians only spoke of spiritual matters to the extent it was expedient to do so. The stars were no longer miraculous and modern technology meant that people no longer needed their guidance; the fleeting comforts of economic prosperity meant that people no longer needed their light.

It was Friedrich Nietzsche who famously declared, 'God is dead'. I would have disagreed, and suggested instead that 'God was away on business'; or, perhaps, that the modern consumer was away on business, and had left God behind. But what business is more important than the spiritual business of infusing into one's life a meaningful cosmological narrative (whether one uses the word God or not)? Apparently, acquiring the right consumer goods was more important, such as a big house with new furniture and the latest television, fashionable clothing, a new car, and the status of prestigious job. Those seemed to have been the objects of ultimate concern in the age of Empire. God forbid one fall behind the Joneses! Given how much collective energy was dedicated to the pursuit of middle-class luxuries, it comes as no surprise to discover that the spiritual sensibility of that age faded.

If these words strike the reader as lacking compassion somewhat, please accept that it is not indifference but anger and frustration that I have been unable to hide. We only get one chance at life, and it pains me that so many were seduced into wasting that chance in pursuit of trinkets and baubles.

♦ ♦ ♦

As I reflected upon this spiritual impoverishment – still lying on the moss-covered log, lost amongst the stars – I found myself strangely thinking about the economist's notion of an 'externality'. An externality is a cost that is not taken into account when determining the market price of something; for example, pollution from a factory may be an 'externality' if the costs of clearing it up fall on society as a whole, rather than on the factory owner who caused it. In such circumstances, the price of the commodity would not reflect the true cost, because the costs of pollution would be 'external' to the price, making the commodities artificially cheap and thus leading to overconsumption. I found this idea illuminating when thinking about the hidden costs of consumer culture; in particular, the cost of spiritual malaise, which was perhaps Empire's greatest externality. In dollar terms, most Westerners were fabulously wealthy when considered in the context of all known history. But how 'rich' would those individuals have been if the costs of spiritual malaise had been factored into the price of economic prosperity? How does one put a price on the absence of God? How would one internalise *that* externality! Needless to say, spiritual well-being defies economic valuation, but that does not mean that it is of no value. On the contrary, it may just mean that spiritual wellbeing is *priceless* and therefore of our highest concern.

♦ ♦ ♦

In my experience, the spiritual search for meaning in life is like climbing a mount. The more one is burdened by superfluous things and concerns, the harder the journey will be, and the more likely it is that one will get lost and never reach the peak. But if one mindfully pares back one's material possessions, keeping only what is necessary for the journey, then this material simplicity will make the path clearer and easier to walk.

This is the paradox of simplicity: less can be more. Unfortunately, humankind's possessive tendencies mean that the benefits of this insight are easily lost. Too often we try to drag all our stuff up the mount, refusing to pare back, without understanding that by giving up some of our precious possessions we will have better things returned to us.

When I let myself be enchanted by ordinary experience, it quickly becomes apparent that the simple life is a profoundly beautiful life, one that is exciting and worth living. For simplicity is nothing if not an affirmative state of mind, an authentic celebration of life – and it is a state of mind that often seems to reflect a mystical appreciation of life, and a deep reverence for nature, even if one does not subscribe to any traditional religion or crude pantheism. The simple life makes mystics of us all.

Earlier generations confronted spiritual questions face to face; too many of us, both past and present, confront those questions through their eyes. But why, as Emerson would insist, should we not also enjoy an original relation to the universe?

♦ ♦ ♦

On the Isle our attitudes toward religion in the traditional sense are liberal, to say the least. There is certainly no 'official' religious or spiritual position, although we do sometimes refer to ourselves as a community of 'seekers', in recognition of the fact that all of us (by virtue of being human) endeavour to weave into our lives a meaningful narrative about our place in the universe. Even the most hard-nosed atheists are spiritual in this sense. After all, to say that the cosmos 'just is' and that it does not require further explanation implicates the atheist in a cosmological thesis, and one no less mind-blowing, surely, than any other explanation. I do not even know what it could mean to say that the cosmos 'just is', any more than I could claim to understand the nature of an omnipotent Creator.

To admit that the origins of the universe are ultimately an unsolvable mystery, beyond the limits of human understanding, should not imply, of course, giving up deep inquiry into those origins. We can still be 'seekers', delving into various spiritual, religious, or secular wisdom traditions in search of nourishing insights, and perhaps even making 'leaps of faith' in one direction or the other. After all, if we close ourselves off from metaphysics, may we not also close ourselves off from the potential benefits of spiritual inquiry? Would that not also be a 'gamble' or 'leap of faith'? On the Isle, our spiritualities have taken on infinitely diverse expressions, and if there were anything in common to them I would say simply that they all represent a thoughtful love of life arising out of an openness to mystery. Above the entrances to our non-denominational Halls of Reverence there are the words: '*THERE IS NOTHING MORE BEAUTIFUL THAN THE MYSTERIOUS*'. That phrase seems to represent our spiritual ethos better than any other.

Nevertheless, owing to our unique history, all the major religions are in fact represented on the Isle, including some new ones, as well as a large minority of atheists, and this diversity of belief systems is not just tolerated but celebrated. One might have thought that this would have set the scene for constant conflict, but generally that is not the case. Despite the divergent religious and non-religious perspectives, there seems to be agreement that there are infinite possible interpretations of one's place in the cosmos, and, furthermore, that there is no independent perspective that could objectively judge the validity of various interpretations. Accordingly, religious positioning on the Isle, and spiritual positioning more generally, is defined first and foremost by a deep and genuine humility – the religious virtue most lacking in the Old World. People may hold their religious or non-religious views passionately, but these views are also held diffidently and with modesty, knowing that there are limits to the human understanding and that one's own take on the universe might turn out to be wrong, however deeply it is experienced as a reflection of the truth. Furthermore, people on the Isle recognise that culturally diverse spiritual or religious narratives generally ask the same 'big questions' about life's meaning, and that we can all learn a great deal from respectfully exploring the various answers that have been given to those questions throughout history. Because of this, we choose not to practise our spiritualities in separate churches or temples, but instead we celebrate their diversity together in our Halls of Reverence, where we gather to meditate, reflect, read, and quietly exchange ideas about the fruits or frustrations of our 'searching'.

Perhaps the most significant reason, however, for why our community can coexist peacefully despite divergent worldviews, is because we share the love of simplicity. The ethos of simple living provides common ground, not only between all major religions and wisdom traditions, but also between traditional political oppositions, and in times of conflict we gather around this idea and look to it for guidance and enlightenment. So far we have been generously rewarded.

♦ ♦ ♦

I wandered internally through these issues as I lay on the fallen tree, but at some stage I must have fallen asleep for an hour, or perhaps two. It did me good, as I awoke feeling fresh and ready for the climb up the mount. It was not a huge mount by any means, although parts were very steep. From past experience I knew that it took roughly three hours to get to the peak, and from the position of the stars I guessed that if I moved at a reasonable pace, I should make the peak by sunrise. Fortunately the full moon made my night climb a safe and pleasant journey.

It turned out that my estimate was accurate. I reached the peak just as the twinkle of dawn emerged on the dark horizon. I watched in awe from my stone seat, exhausted from the long walk and steep climb, but energised by the prospect of what was unfolding before my eyes. The spectacular light from this golden dawn began colouring the skies with slowly moving hues of red, pink, purple, and blue, and the light also began highlighting the vast green landscapes and blue seas that surrounded me. The mountain face spread out below me like a dark cloak and disappeared into the surrounding hills and forests. The land was delicately carved up with sparkling rivers that occasionally swelled into smooth lakes reflecting the fiery skies. The birds began to sing their praises to a world that seemed to be in perfect harmony.

The universe was waking up and as it did so I found myself awakening with it. A cosmological wind strengthened within me, blowing new energy onto the embers of my soul and casting renewed light upon my world. I felt infinitely grateful to be alive and present to this extraordinary scene. Standing there I experienced an ecstatic moment of rapture, through which, for a moment, at least, I felt in perfect unity with the universe. I felt perfectly safe, blessed to be in a world radiating such beauty, grandeur, power, and mystery. It may have been fleeting, but such moments of mystical madness are so intense that one is never the same again. They shape the soul in ways that cannot be undone.

I was reminded again of the words of Emerson:

> *I see the spectacle of morning from the hilltop over against my house, from daybreak to sunrise, with emotions which an angel might share. The long slender bars of cloud float like fishes in the sea of crimson light. From the earth, as a shore, I look out into that silent sea. I seem to partake its rapid transformations; the active enchantment reaches my dust, and I dilate and conspire with the morning wind.*

As my trance slowly loosened its grip on me, I found that my mind was drawn to the question of utopia. What was the nature of the good society? And could it be realised? As I looked over Entropia from my privileged perspective on the mount, the sun slowly rising over this land I called home, I asked myself whether we had in fact achieved something unique in the history of humankind; something close to the goal for which the march of history had implicitly aimed. Was our society one that respected the deep future? Had we created the social, economic, and political conditions that maximised human creativity and happiness? On both counts, I suspected it was indeed so.

♦ ♦ ♦

From the moment I left my abode in the village, my mind had been furiously at work, attempting to sort out the debris of my discontent in order to rebuild my composure. I knew that a tranquil consciousness required effort and self-discipline, and I was prepared to labour for it – for my own sake, and for the sake of others. Tranquillity and angst are both contagious, so it matters which of them we feed.

Having meditated my way though an array of my troubles on the march to the peak, and having just been overwhelmed by the sublime vista of the Isle at dawn, I had expected that my insides, at last, would have been at rest; that I would have found my peace. I had even turned my back on the spectacular view and taken a few steps down the mount, presuming that my pilgrimage was over and that it was time to return home. But with every step I took, my insides burned more furiously. Had I missed something fundamental? Should I return to the peak and take a second look? It was if the mount were urging me to confront the ultimate depths of my conscience and face the real questions that had driven me away from the village, the questions that were still festering beneath the surface of my consciousness.

I stopped in my path, and noticed as I returned to the peak that I was trembling slightly and covered in a cold sweat. The view of the Isle now looked different, although in ways I could not yet decipher or articulate clearly. For an instant the skies looked like the thin film of a bubble that had encapsulated our tiny Isle, a bubble floating alone in the ether, complete unto itself. I suddenly realised that by clearing away the internal debris surrounding my thoughts, I had merely exposed the underlying issue that had subconsciously sent my insides into disarray in the first place. I found myself terrified by my own thoughts, afraid to acknowledge them.

But acknowledge them I did. As I stared out over the land of Entropia I came to understand that however broad my perspective might have seemed from the mount, it remained confined within a disturbing frame of reference – confined within the bubble into which I had been born. There I had been, just moments before, looking out upon the Isle as if it were the whole world. Yet it was not the whole world, but only a tiny fragment of it! How could I ever expect to understand 'the part' or even 'my part in the part', without reference to 'the whole'? Our entire community on the Isle was guilty of embracing this narrow prospect of reality, falsely identifying the Isle with the cosmos. It was the unspoken assumption that none of us had ever dared to question. It was just taken as given that the Great Disruption had isolated the Isle from the rest of humankind *permanently*. But, of course, a moment's honest consideration made it clear that our isolation had become a choice, not something externally imposed upon us by force of circumstances. If we had wanted to leave the Isle, we could have easily built a ship. In fact, we already had a ship anchored off the southeast coast (the one that had delivered us consumer waste all those years ago). This vessel simply needed refuelling with biofuel to once again become functional. At some stage in recent history, then, our community had *chosen* isolation, even if we never dared to articulate that choice.

But what were the ethics of this voluntary isolation? Granted, when our isolation was imposed upon us due to the Great Disruption, there was arguably no ethical issue at hand, because it was proper for us to work toward securing our own survival. When one is at risk of starvation, one does not worry about how people on the other side of world are going to feed themselves. One worries about staying warm and producing local food for family, friends, and community. In fact, at first there was really no other option for us. That mindset of self-reliance and self-provision, however, had become rather uncritically entrenched in recent decades, despite circumstances changing. As I gazed over the Isle from the mount's peak, I began to wonder about our duties to the rest of humanity, given that the material foundations of our way of life were now firmly established and secured.

What if humanity was in desperate need of assistance? It was highly likely, almost certain, that the rest of humanity had not made its way through the Great Disruption as prosperously as our own community. Perhaps we could be of service? Our small numbers would obviously limit our capacity to assist, but if we could reduce suffering even in one small corner of the earth, was it not our duty to do so? Were we justified in 'making art' in comfortable isolation while the rest of the world suffered? I realised that the completion of my latest composition had engendered these questions deep in my soul – so deep that it took my march to the mount to bring them to the surface.

And so it was that I returned to the village with the intention of drafting an open letter to the councils, through which I would raise the ethical issue of our isolation. I felt obliged to invite my community to consider whether some of us, at least, should leave the Isle in order to assess the state of civilisation, and to consider whether our duties now reached beyond our own borders. It was not that I had reached any firm conclusions about how these questions should be answered. I only knew that they ought to be asked and taken seriously.

As it turned out, however, soon after I returned from the mount, a series of events took place that resulted in my letter never being written.

7

The Noble Lie

Societies never expect the timing or the form of their greatest turning points. This was certainly the case for those of us on the Isle, who could not possibly have anticipated the twist that would come to define our own tale. It was in all other ways an ordinary autumn day; the sun had risen and fallen like any other. But in rising and falling with such inescapable consistency we now see that the sun was mimicking the cycle of civilisation itself, as if trying to tell us something about our own future.

Two poets, Ludwig and Zara, were walking on the western beach, near the Great Caves, when they had sat down on the warm sand dunes intending to watch the sun set. Having become engrossed in a friendly but passionate disagreement about the literary value of an old book of verse, they did not even see the ship appear on the clear horizon. As the winds and moon rose slowly, the ship was drawn inward, and only as the two interlocutors stood to begin their journey homeward did they notice the mysterious vessel drifting quietly toward the shore. In stunned silence they watched it approach the beach through dark, sparkling waters.

Ever since the Great Disruption, Entropia had not received a single visitor, not even any cargo ships. The community had lived self-sufficiently in perfect isolation, and the recent generations, especially the present one, had grown up thinking that this would always be so; that the world of their childhoods would endure endlessly into the future.

Seeing this strange vessel drift in from beyond, therefore, was almost like watching the laws of physics bend before one's very eyes. It could not possibly be happening, and yet it was.

Should they return to the village and inform the councils? Should they hide amongst the trees and watch on from afar? What were they to do? With bloodless faces reflecting the blue-grey moonlight, Ludwig and Zara stared out upon this simple but surreal scene, remaining paralysed by fear and indecision as the ship anchored about fifty metres offshore. A small boat was lowered carefully into the waters, and what looked like a single individual jumped aboard and began rowing toward the shore. Zara was first to move, stepping slowly toward the water's edge, as if in a trance. Ludwig, his mind racing, soon followed in cautious support. Surely their eyes were deceiving them.

'Warm greetings,' a man's voice bellowed out from afar, the silhouette holding up a lantern near his face, as if to expose himself as a comrade. The stranger then returned to work his oars and the rowboat edged unevenly toward the shore. Eventually, as the small vessel ran up against its limits in the sand, the man hopped overboard and dropped a small anchor into the shallow waters. With tidy, silver hair, he looked to be in his mid-fifties, and was dressed in a new suit and tie, the elegance of which clashed with his gumboots that were unsuccessfully keeping his pants dry. Knee deep in the quietly lapping tide, he turned to look at the two still silhouettes on the shore.

'I am sure my presence comes as a great shock,' the stranger continued, without approaching further. 'But I assure you my motives are peaceful, so please be at ease.' Although his voice was calm and kind, Ludwig and Zara remained motionless and silent on the hard, damp sand, still muted by the fact that their minds were insane with activity. 'My name is Jacob,' the stranger offered.

After what seemed like the passing of several tides, Ludwig's timorous voice broke the silence. 'My name is Ludwig,' he began hesitantly, 'this is Zara. We have not had visitors on this Isle for... for... for generations. So, yes, brother, with respect, your presence certainly comes as a shock to us. Who are you and where are you from? And what are you doing here?'

'I have much to explain, and will do so,' the man answered promptly, 'but may I first step ashore so that I can shake your hands and see your faces on dry land? I have been at sea for longer than I would have liked, my friends, and would be grateful now to stand upon solid ground again. And this water is cold.' Intuitively satisfied that this man was not a physical threat to them, Ludwig and Zara invited him ashore and greeted him with the handshake he sought. His eyes were honest, but alien, and somehow reflecting the burdens of another world.

He said that he had a message to deliver.

♦ ♦ ♦

The journey back to the village was long and slow, with Ludwig and Zara raining questions down upon this man Jacob Walters, who had appeared as if from nowhere out of the darkness of night. With compassion and artfulness, Mr Walters took pains to convey his message to them in a way that was as psychologically digestible as possible, although he knew that nothing could change the fact that his story would shake the foundations of Entropia. He answered the questions posed to him as best he could, and his questioners did their best to absorb the extraordinary words he spoke.

Not really knowing how to respond to the deeply unsettling message that Mr Walters bore, and to some extent incredulous, Ludwig and Zara tentatively decided that the most appropriate course of action would be to take Mr

Walters to one of their own abodes, where they could all rest until the next morning. There was no point waking the community with the moon so high in the sky, and the small group managed to reach Ludwig's hut, it being the closer, without crossing paths with any other members of the community. They each had a piece of bread and a glass of water, then quietly organised their sleeping arrangements. There would be time to talk tomorrow.

When they rose with the sun the next day, all three confessed to having slept little, if at all, which was hardly surprising, given the circumstances, tired though they all were. After a short discussion it was agreed that Ludwig would stay with Mr Walters in the hut, while Zara would set about organising and publicising a town meeting. They felt that the only moral course of action was to share with the community the message that had been delivered the evening before, and that was indeed Mr Walters' desire. 'That is why I have come,' he said, with stern resignation.

Within a few hours, rumours of the mysterious vessel near the caves had already filtered throughout the community. Speculations abounded about where the vessel had come from and to whom it might belong. Knowing that some answers had to be provided without delay, Zara had discreetly posted several notices around the village that simply advised people that someone would be addressing the entire community at the amphitheatre at midday, and that all questions regarding the vessel would be answered then. 'EVERYONE MUST ATTEND – NO EXCEPTIONS', the notice implored, with unprecedented assertiveness.

Naturally, the Isle was abuzz with mystery, anticipation, and for a short time a certain degree of apprehension, even fear. By the time midday came, however, a broad consensus had formed that this meeting must be an elaborate play put on by one of the Schools of Art, and that the community was to be treated with a special performance of some sort. Some conjectured that a fellow called Silentio was behind the event, although he was most surprised (and a little flattered) when that groundless rumour met his ears.

There would indeed be a spectacle, but this was no aesthetic hoax, as everyone would soon discover.

♦ ♦ ♦

A crowd began gathering around eleven thirty, and before long it seemed the entire community was present, each individual slowly finding a seat in the amphitheatre that had been constructed masterfully by the first generation. It was an extraordinary scene in an extraordinary place. The air was alive with curiosity and speculation, and still nobody had any idea who was behind this unusual event. For some time the stage remained empty, which only heightened the electric mood of tense excitement.

Eventually, just as the crowd seemed to be getting a little restless, Ludwig and Zara took to the stage and waited side by side as the atmospheric murmur faded away into silence. In the distance a flock of rainbow lorikeets chattered incessantly to each other, and frogs could be heard in the small pond nearby; toward the back a newborn let out a short cry, and somewhere an old man coughed; there was some shuffling of feet on the stone terraces. But otherwise the land of Entropia was quiet and perfectly attentive.

'Thank you all for meeting here at such short notice,' Zara began, her quiet but melodic voice reaching the most distant seats in the full amphitheatre with ease. 'We appreciate that you have all put aside your plans or routines to be here, but you can be sure that this meeting deserves the urgency with which it has been given. There are matters of unique social importance that must be shared with you all at once.'

At this stage Zara turned to Ludwig, who was clearly intimidated by the situation in which he found himself. The crowd was murmuring apprehensively to itself in a state of confusion. Breathing deeply, Ludwig took a timid step forward and paused to gather his thoughts before addressing the crowd, whose murmur once again fell into silence. 'My fellow citizens,' he began, speaking slowly and deliberately, 'many of you have already heard rumours that a foreign ship has anchored off the Western beach near the caves. For those who have not walked to see it for themselves, let me confirm that this is indeed so, having witnessed the vessel with my own eyes. Some of you have speculated that this vessel might be the work of some group of artists who wish to play aesthetic games with us, but I must tell you at once, friends, for fear of being misunderstood, that we are not here today to play any games. Not at all. We have all gathered here because... our Isle has received a visitor.'

The amphitheatre was silent. For the first time it was dawning on the crowd that this event was not something arranged by the Schools of Art. Could it be, people began asking themselves, that there really was a foreign vessel in Entropian waters? Had the Isle indeed received a visitor from beyond? Everything became unambiguously real when the visitor himself, who had been waiting behind a stone pillar to the side of the stage, appeared to face the audience he sought.

Zara motioned toward their unfamiliar visitor, offering him the briefest introduction as he made his way across the stage in conspicuously foreign garb. 'Fellow citizens,' she said, 'allow me to introduce Jacob Walters, who arrived on the Isle late yesterday evening. He comes bearing a message that he wishes to deliver to us, presently. Please dignify our visitor with your closest attention.' She paused with disquiet in her eyes, before adding, almost in a whisper: 'Hold onto your seats'.

On saying these words, Zara followed Ludwig off stage to leave their visitor alone before his audience.

♦ ♦ ♦

In accordance with protocol, the proceedings of this particular town meeting were recorded by an appointed scribe, which means that the words spoken by Jacob Walters can be reproduced here verbatim. As I was present at this defining event, I can confirm that what follows is a true and accurate statement of what was said. Mr Walters' words speak for themselves and therefore require little commentary from me.

He cleared his throat and began to speak:

> I cannot imagine what must be running through your minds at the moment, but if you will indulge me for a while I will endeavour to answer some of the questions that I can only assume you must have. For several months I have known that this occasion lay before me – the day when I would have to address you all – and every night I have gone over in my head, one thousand times, how best to convey the message that I bring you today. But every night, including my sleepless night just passed, I was unable to craft the delicate speech that I was seeking. I now know that what I sought was impossible, for there is no easy or delicate way to deliver the message I bear. Consequently, I stand before you now feeling wholly unprepared, and am left with no option but to start from the beginning and to express as coherently as I can what I have come here to say. There will be time for questions when I am done, and I am sure there will be many. For now, please listen.
>
> My name, as you already know, is Jacob Walters, and last evening I sailed into your waters alone, on the

vessel that lies just off the western beach. I know that your community has lived in complete isolation for many decades, so I can only try to understand how unsettling it must be for a visitor to suddenly appear on your shores, unannounced and requesting an opportunity to address your community. It was never my intention to startle you. But please accept that I am here because I have to be here, in ways and for reasons that I shall try to explain.

You will be wondering from where I have come, so let me begin there. I sailed to your shores from the North Island of New Zealand, whose government I serve by being here today. It is a service that weighs heavily upon me, for the operation in which I have found myself involved rests upon questionable grounds, and the only thing that gives me peace today is knowing that at last the truth can be spoken and that the 'noble lie', as we have come to call it, can be revealed.

Please bear with me. What I am about to say will doubtless be received by you in various ways, but I suspect that a mixture of anger, confusion, and disbelief will be amongst the flurry of emotions which you experience. I ask that you prepare as best you can to hear things that I am afraid will turn your world upside down. And while I am prepared to accept whatever might befall me upon delivering this message, please understand that however questionable my government's actions might have been, the ideals that motivated us throughout were shaped by a love of humanity and a genuine desire to advance the human condition. Whether that 'end' justifies our 'means' is a question that I have struggled with in the depths of my soul, but as yet have been unable to resolve. At times I have felt that our actions have been justifiable in relation to some conception of the 'greater good', which we believe to be serving; at other times – perhaps, if I am honest, most of the time – I have been haunted by the suspicion that the entire operation is and has always been unforgivable, no matter how noble our intentions might have been. At the end of the day, however, I suppose my own view of the matter is of no significance. You will arrive at your own verdict and ultimately face the decision of how to respond. But first I must deliver my message.

The narrative I am here to convey today begins in 1945, at the close of the Second World War. The world was in the throes of dealing with the aftermath of humankind's bloodiest and most destructive war, and in most places, including my own country, the focus was primarily on getting the domestic economy up and running again. There were some people, however, who were questioning whether the return of a functioning industrial economy was really the goal for which our nation, or indeed the world, should be aiming. After all, these critics asked, had not the limitless pursuit of wealth and power been what drove the world to war in the first place? Was not war, both internal and external, inherent to the very nature of industrial civilisation? Moreover, had not the holocaust, the Gulags, and the atom bomb, provided compelling grounds to doubt whether a harmonious industrial civilisation was even a theoretical possibility? Some resigned themselves to the fact that a civilisation at war both with itself and the planet was the best humankind could hope for – the best we deserved. Others dreamed of an alternative way.

As it happened, one of our Members of Parliament in New Zealand had come to the conclusion – hardly an original conclusion, I should add – that the materialistic values underpinning industrial civilisation were actually the deepest and primary causes of the world's military conflicts, and that any hope for peace on a planet of finite resources depended on the emergence of some fundamentally alternative, non-materialistic way of life; a way of life based, at the very least, on voluntarily restrained resource consumption. He felt that attempting to reform industrial civilisation was not an adequate response to the horrors it brought; he felt something 'wholly other' needed to be created, or at least experimented with.

This parliamentarian happened to be extremely wealthy, being the beneficiary of a huge inheritance, and based on his private musings he offered to fund and coordinate a government-sanctioned 'experiment in living', provided one of the nation's most isolated wildlife reserves in the South Pacific Ocean could be made available. To cut a long story short, the New Zealand government was being invited by this eccentric individual to facilitate the creation of some form of utopian community, in the hope of shedding some light on perennial questions about 'good economy' and the nature of human co-existence. The proposal was convincingly presented, peculiar though it was, and ultimately it was approved behind the closed doors of the Department of Internal Affairs, with only a very small handful of individuals being privy to the decision. Before long, secret preparations for the experiment began. The project became known as Operation Walden, after Henry Thoreau's simple living manifesto that best embodied its non-materialistic values.

You will have already noticed, I am sure, the similarities between this experiment in living and the history you have come to know of your own community's origins. I must inform you now, however, that these similarities are not merely coincidental; they are in fact actually different versions of the same story. The challenge that I face is explaining to you all why it is that the history I have just described is actually your community's *true* history, and that the history you learnt as children is actually a fabrication, a story created as part of my government's experiment with utopia – the experiment in which you have all been unknowing participants. I will not pretend to understand how unsettling it must be to hear this, and I suspect that my words are testing the limits of your credulity. But let me continue.

The story of Mortimer Flynn, which I know you are all intimately familiar with, was actually written by a gifted young intern in the Department of Internal Affairs, who occasionally was employed as a ghost-writer for various parliamentarians due to his literary abilities and cultural insight. When the Department's preparations were getting underway for the utopian living experiment, this intern was asked to concoct a history of the experiment that did not admit to any government involvement. Rightly or wrongly, it was thought that the experiment would work best if the participants thought that the island community arose more organically, rather than being the product of a governmental initiative. The story of Mortimer Flynn was sufficient for this purpose. The first generation on the Isle was taught this artificial history, knowing it to be artificial, and they then raised their children accordingly – for the good of a cause they obviously believed in. That history has been passed down as fact ever since.

As one can no doubt imagine, Mr Walters' words held the community's attention, heavy though his revelations were in meaning and significance. This was not the time to let our minds wander! But if we thought the challenging narrative was over, we were mistaken. Our visitor's slowly spoken sentences continued to place an almost unbearable demand on us:

> Confronting though these disclosures will be, good people, I am afraid that there is still more to my message. In order to ensure that participants on the island did not have the inclination to leave, further historical events were concocted. The most effective means the Department could come up with for keeping participants on the island was to make the world beyond its borders seem terrifying, dangerous, and chaotic. To this end it was decided that the participants must believe that civilisation had collapsed, and that violence, famine, and disease were what they would find should they ever leave the island. It turned out to be an effective enough story, but it is just that – a story.
>
> In other words, what I am telling you – difficult though it will be to believe or even understand – is that the history of civilisation's collapse, which you have all learned in your schools, is actually just a fictional scenario developed by that same intern who crafted the story of Mortimer Flynn. In fact, that intern, who by this stage was a senior advisor to the Department, wrote a short essay on the hypothetical collapse, which the Department decided to circulate anonymously amongst your community as a teaching tool, and which I understand is still read widely today. In retrospect, the essay was extraordinarily prescient, building into its story consumerist and environmentalist themes that were, at the time, only just beginning to emerge on the intellectual fringe. But for better or for worse, I tell you, civilisation beyond these borders today is still very much alive – at least for the time being, and I will have

more to say about the present situation shortly. Before moving on, however, I must finish revealing the difficult truths that burden me.

This is the point at which I fear your cosmology will be truly disturbed, if it is not already, so please brace yourself for further impact. When working out the details of Operation Walden, the Department of Internal Affairs arrived at the opinion that, to be plausible, the fictional collapse of civilisation, which was to be taught in the schools of history on this island, should take place well into the future. The reasoning was that if civilisation could endure a war as horrendous as the one that ended in 1945, then it was a robust civilisation that could not easily be dissolved by way of fictional collapse. Accordingly, in order to make that fictional collapse as believable a possible, it was felt that many years of civilisational deterioration would have to occur before any collapse could plausibly take place. That, at least, was the official reason for the collapse taking place in the future. Unofficially, some suspect that the individuals who were in charge of the operation had a 'God complex,' of sorts, and just wanted to push the boundaries of their control over the situation to the hilt. Whatever the case, the collapse of civilisation was written into your history, but decades into the future, and this is the false history you have all been taught. In short, the stories of Mortimer Flynn and the collapse of civilisation make up the 'noble lie' that the Department felt it needed to tell in order to maximise the chances of the experiment's success and longevity. As I said earlier, it was felt the end justified the means; at least, that is what we have always told ourselves in order to get to sleep at night.

What this means for your place in history is perfectly clear to *me*, but so bizarre must my words sound to you,

> if they can be absorbed at all, that I feel I should elaborate in order to ensure that I make myself clear. Let me put it this way. Your history lessons have taught you that Mortimer Flynn's Entropia experiment was launched in 1934, and that civilisation collapsed toward the end of the third decade of the 21st century. Given that there have been three generations since that fictional 'collapse', it makes perfect sense that you believe that we are living in the year 2099. But what I am telling you is that you have been educated into a myth – by a first generation that was necessarily complicit in the myth – and that in matter of fact, Operation Walden, which was launched in 1945, is barely three generations old. During the period of this operation my government has monitored your society, first through covert radio contact with certain members of the first generation, and more recently with satellite surveillance. Put as clearly and as succinctly as possible, then, I am here to tell you that Entropia is a government-sanctioned living experiment; that civilisation has not collapsed; and that we are, in fact, as I speak these words, living on the 4th day of February, in the year 2013.

At this stage I should briefly interrupt the speech of Mr Walters again, if only to allow the reader to absorb his astonishing message. One might like to imagine being in my position on that day, or the position of any of my peers, listening to these words as the foundations of our world collapsed beneath us. Try as one might, however, any attempt to understand the existential earthquake we all experienced that day will necessarily fail. We were stunned to the point of paralysis, and words simply cannot convey our sense of temporal dislocation. I am sure that I was not the only one who felt dangerously close to the edge of insanity.

I can remember vividly my own train of thoughts during this explosive occasion, thoughts which immediately turned to my childhood. I thought about how I used to sit with my grandparents, who would tell stories about the Old World and how it had degenerated into barbarism. If what Jacob Walters was saying was true, my grandparents, now long deceased, were of the first generation on the Isle, and were accordingly aware of the 'noble lie' which had just been revealed. They, too, must have believed in the 'greater good' that their stories were attempting to serve, and were prepared to educate their grandchildren, as they had educated their children, according to a fabricated account of history.

On hearing Mr Walters' words I recall my first emotions were a mixture of rage and humiliation. How dare anyone assume the right to treat me as a lab rat in their experiment! My initial impulse was that no end could justify these means, simply as a matter of human dignity. As my rational side took control, however, my mind turned to scepticism, casting doubt upon the possibility that what I had just heard could actually be true. Surely someone was playing games with us; surely there were holes in this tall tale that would expose Mr Walters as a fraud. But as I worked my way through his story, I found it at every point consistent with my lived experience. I realised that even the great fire in the library, which we were taught about in school, must have been concocted to explain the fact that there were no written records or books relating to the first eras in our history. The absence of such records and books was always spoken about with such regret on the Isle, and we lamented, in particular, the fact that we had no memoirs from our ancestors to give us a deeper insight into the history of our community on the Isle. We were told that the memoirs that had existed were burnt to ashes. But now, on the basis of what we had just heard, there was no longer any reason to lament the loss of such records, because such records never existed. There were no generations on the Isle prior to my grandparent's era, and so there could be no records of them.

To those who were not educated into our fabricated history, it may seem strange that we were so accepting of it. But this sense of strangeness can only arise out of a failure to appreciate how easily children are educated into a form of life, first sitting upon someone's knee, and then through lessons ratified by wider society. Such lessons are the basis upon which a worldview is established and entrenched. The most fundamental aspects of any worldview are rarely subjected to critical examination, because those aspects provide the background intellectual structure within which critical examination attempts to take place. In order to begin thinking critically about the world, some things have to be taken for granted. As it was, our community took history for granted.

But enough of my own reactions and thoughts, which are merely incidental to this historical account and are intended only to illuminate it. Let us now return to Mr Walters' speech, for there were several important issues that he had not yet touched upon but which required, and in time received, an explanation:

> So there you have it, the 'noble lie' revealed. For what it is worth, I am deeply sorry for the distress my words will surely cause you; for the distress I can see they are already causing some of you. But now is not the time, I suspect, for me to seek your forgiveness, with emotions running so high and so many questions still unanswered. Furthermore, while there might be an occasion for us to debate the justifiability of my government's actions – actions of which I have played an intimate part – I am acutely aware that this is not the time for me to attempt to defend our living

experiment; or, rather, your living experiment. There is, however, one question that I am sure you are waiting to have answered, and that is: why have I been directed to reveal these things to you? Perhaps more specifically: why *now*? Answering this question is in fact the second task my government has assigned to me, and a task which I will now attempt to fulfil. Permit me a moment, if you will, to provide something of a preface to my answer.

The German philosopher Georg Hegel once remarked that the events of history repeat themselves, as it were, twice, to which Karl Marx added: 'the first time as tragedy, the second as farce'. For reasons I must now explain, those of us involved in Operation Walden have come to suspect that Hegel and Marx were right in saying these things, only that the first historical occurrence is a farce, to be followed by a tragic repetition. What I mean to suggest by this is that the farcical history of civilisational collapse that you were taught in your schools is, as I speak, in the process of repeating itself as a tragic reality. That is to say, your fictional history is proving to be not so far from the truth after all – and becoming truer by the day.

This situation has presented those of us in the Department who are involved in Operation Walden with something of a dilemma. We have watched on from a distance as your society has flourished peacefully beyond historical precedent, and we have compiled extensive notes on the most important features of your social, economic, and political structures, as well as your extraordinary cultural and artistic advances. It was always our intention to let the experiment continue indefinitely, for we were convinced that there was still much to be gained from observing from afar your unique community – your existing Utopia. But as our civilisation continues to deteriorate to the point where it is now threatening to collapse, and as it degrades ever-more violently the ecosystems upon which the entire community of life depends, it has dawned upon us that perhaps our dying civilisation can only be saved by the lessons your community has already learned. More pragmatically, our government can no longer afford to dedicate personnel to this operation, as our economy, and the global economy, continues its economic nosedive. Accordingly, after much deliberation, the Department decided that it would be wholly unjustifiable to sit by and let civilisation collapse, with all the suffering this would entail, when perhaps the key to a just, sustainable, and flourishing world was already within our grasp. Arguably we have kept your existence secret from the world too long already. Time certainly seems to be running out, which is why, in the end, I am here.

Like Plato sheepishly inviting the poets back after banishing them from his Republic, I am here to say that civilisation desperately needs you to emerge from isolation and help us rebuild our civilisation according to the 'simpler ways' of Entropia. That is the invitation I have been instructed to deliver, and with this task now complete, I leave you with the question of how you ought to respond.

◆ ◆ ◆

The Isle of Furor Poeticus was never the same again. How could it be, having heard all this? I remember the eerie silence that followed the closing of Mr Walters' speech like it was yesterday; there was a soft, cool wind that provided the only sense of movement in our world. It was as if even the wildlife had been taken aback. Nothing moved. Nobody knew what to do or say.

Finally – mercifully – Ludwig returned to the stage and suggested that Mr Walters remain on the island for a week or so in order to answer the most pressing questions that remained outstanding, a proposition that was to receive the support both of the community and Mr Walters. During this period it was agreed that the community would meet regularly and at length to discuss how it should respond to the message that it had just received.

8

More Day to Dawn

In the end, the question we were left with upon receiving Mr Walters' message was the question of whether to continue living happily in our harmonious, aesthetic bubble, in the middle of the South Pacific Ocean, and hope that the imminent disintegration of Empire would not interfere with our quiet corner of Earth; or, enter the world of Empire with our story of simplicity and try, if it may be so put, to show the fly of civilisation the way out of its bottle. Even if we did return to the 'Old World', however, it was hardly certain that our story would be enough to change the trajectory of civilisation. After all, when has reason ever been enough for humankind to act? We are anything but rational, evidence-based creatures. What is more, flies are arguably better dead than shown the way out of the bottle. It seemed the questions with which we were faced were complex ones, pulling us in various directions at once.

Thus the debate began about what our community should do and how we should respond. At first the issue of whether to stay on the Isle or go split the community more or less down the middle. Those who advocated remaining in isolation on the Isle were generally those who felt most aggrieved by the deception that lay at the foundation of Operation Walden. What did any of us owe a civilisation that treated us as lab rats in its desperate experiment? Was not the 'noble lie', so-called, just one more example of a civilisation treating human beings as means not as ends in themselves? And is the 'ignoble lie' of affluence any different? Why not stay in Entropia, the Republic of Ends? In the eyes of many, the invitation to leave the Isle to assist civilisation did not wash well at all, and I admit with some embarrassment that at first my own kneejerk reaction was that we should stay on the Isle out of spite, civilisation be damned.

Arguments in favour of rejecting the invitation were supported by the horrendous stories we began to hear about the existing nature of Empire; stories of cruelty, arrogance, apathy, and astonishing blindness and stupidity. 'That civilisation does not deserve to exist!' shouted one citizen during the first town meeting after the noble lie was exposed. 'Let it fall, for Earth's sake, and let it take our species down with it!' shouted another. These sentiments were not easily calmed, and with emotions inflamed by all that had been said in the amphitheatre, the arguments in favour of staying on the Isle found many vocal and dogmatic supporters.

There was also another line of argument, based in aesthetics, which some felt provided further grounds for staying put. In the second or third meeting a well-known, elderly aesthete stood up and asserted, in all seriousness, that he could not possibly return to civilisation on the grounds that 'it was far too ugly, in all respects'. His argument was blunt and crudely expressed, but it was developed in more sophisticated ways by others. 'If it were the case that a civilisation as obscene as Empire cannot be saved,' one individual asked rhetorically, 'would it not be our duty to live the life we have imagined right here, until the wick of civilisation burns itself dead?'. This aesthetic positioning essentially held that artistic activity, broadly defined, is humankind's highest calling, and that our community therefore should create in an aesthetic frenzy until the End of Days. It would be quite a way to go, would it not? A different and perhaps more robust thread in the same line of thinking held that in a world, such as the present one, that entailed such deep and unspeakable suffering, human beings were justified in seeking whatever solace they could find in the practice or contemplation of art. In dark times, a moment's respite, if it is on offer, is an almost irresistible temptation.

Weighty though some of these and other arguments were, the longer our discussions endured the more people came to see that staying on the Isle while Empire entered its terminal decline would be rather like fiddling while Rome burned. Granted, the living experiment in which we were unknowing participants violated basic ethical standards, but at the same time, it seemed to be the case that those coordinating Operation Walden sincerely felt that they were serving the greater good – and it was confronting to realise that arguably they were. In order to develop better ways to live, people must be prepared to experiment with the present ways. If that is indeed so, the utilitarian must condone their actions as proper, even if those actions appear subjectively wrong to those who were deceived by them. Those of us who grew up on the Isle, however, will probably always lack the psychological distance to assess the propriety of the experiment with any level of objectivity. Whatever the case, presently we must let the issue of Operation Walden's justifiability remain an open question, to be addressed in more depth if a suitable occasion ever arises. Personally I am not so sure it is worth debating, which is to say, what is done, is done.

As for the argument that Empire did not deserve our assistance, well, this line of reasoning, intuitively powerful though it was, made the unjustified assumption that the ones who would suffer most if civilisation collapsed would be the ones responsible for the collapse. The fact is, however, that the poorest and most disadvantaged are almost always the ones who suffer most in times of social upheaval, despite being least responsible for the destabilising conditions.

Consequently, our return to civilisation, some argued, should not be driven by the saintly motivation to protect the elite classes from their own wrongdoings; that would be far too much to expect, even from a saint. Rather, it should be driven by the humanitarian desire to do what we could to save those who were, if not innocent, then at least much less culpable. As one young speaker put it, 'we should die trying to build a flourishing, simple, low-energy civilisation – not because we think we will succeed, but because if we do not do what we can, something noble in our hearts and spirits will be lost'. This was the burden of our privilege, and realising as much probably represented the turning point in our long discussions.

I should point out that there was a small minority that held fast to the validity of the aesthetic arguments, as no one was quite able to formulate a rebuttal that was not itself susceptible to deconstruction. It turned out, however, the justifiability of those arguments did not have to be determined, as such, for the following reason. Although the vast majority of our community ultimately came to the decision that leaving the Isle was our duty, there were certain realities that some members of our community had to face, most notably, the elderly. These oldest members of our community had entered a phase in life where their frailty meant that they could not be expected to serve as activists, and so it was suggested that at least these members, numbering a little over one hundred, would remain on the Isle. But given that they would be unable to undertake all the physical work needed to sustain the economy, the committed aesthetes, also numbering around one hundred, decided that they would remain on the Isle too. They would provide the basic labour needed to provide a dignified standard of living for the community which remained, and in return for this social service, they would be free to spend the best part of their days engaging in – indulging, some would say – their artistic endeavours, as they had always done.

Consequently, after almost two weeks of deliberation, it was decided that around seventeen hundred and fifty of us would leave the Isle to take up residence in our new home – an industrial civilisation in decline. The New Zealand government was good enough to provide us with a temporary residence in one of its unused army barracks, and it helped coordinate our integration into the new reality in which we found ourselves suddenly immersed. The bubble we had been living in had well and truly burst. For the first time we experienced the rawness of real life: the sound of police cars; the absence of a place to call home; and most of all, deep uncertainty about the future. I am sure we must have looked like deer in the headlights of this fast-approaching 'New World'.

Over recent months most of us have moved away from the barracks into various cities and towns around the world. Memories of life on the Isle already are growing dimmer and more distant, as if it were all but a dream. My peers and I have begun the work that has been asked of us, doing what we can to highlight the fundamental importance of material simplicity to a just, sustainable, and flourishing civilisation. I, for one, have acquired a part-time post as a university lecturer, dedicating most of my efforts to unpacking the philosophical and evidential foundations of Entropia's 'simpler way'. As well as trying to build resilience with my local community in the face of forthcoming shocks, I am also trying to write a book of creative non-fiction about the simple but fulfilling lives of Plato's banished poets. I hope that this mythical example will provide something of a guiding light to our lost civilisation, like a morning star that offers direction at a new dawn. Progress is slow and uneven on all counts, but every now and then I see signs that the sparks of simplicity are beginning to burn brighter. If you see any such sparks, gentle reader, please blow on the embers, light a torch, and pass the flame on.

We are all in this together.

Epilogue

Industrial civilisation is at a point in history where it is faced with the pressing issue of whether it can afford the cost of its own existence. Like a growing number of others, I do not believe that it can afford this, at least, not for much longer. Overlapping crises are currently plaguing the world – financial, ecological, cultural, and spiritual – and these crises present all of us living within industrial civilisation with the question of how best to respond to the threat of collapse. Are we going to open our eyes, muster all the courage we can find, and move decisively toward a simpler, less energy-intensive way of life? Or are we going to let things burn to the ground with heads in sand, as the tide moves in? The choice is ours to make, which correctly implies that however burdened we might be by the chains of industrialisation, we remain free enough to build an alternative, if that is what we want; if that is what we choose to fight for.

We are hardly the first civilisation, of course, to be faced with the prospect of collapse. All previous civilisations have faced it – and have been inadequate to the task. But perhaps we can be the first to understand the dynamics at play. Perhaps we can even respond in such a way as to avoid the collapse scenario that has marked the end of all other civilisations. There is some real work ahead of us, however, both with our heads and our hands. In order to respond effectively, more people must understand the magnitude of overlapping global problems and their underlying causes, otherwise we will find ourselves hacking at the branches of those problems, when we must be focusing on the roots. To begin with, this will involve recognising that industrial civilisation cannot be fixed but must be replaced, on the grounds that it is driven by a growth imperative that is running up against the social, economic, and ecological limits to growth, with consequences that are unfolding more catastrophically by the day. Technology cannot save industrial civilisation from itself, and the goal of globalising affluence is a suicide pact that must be rejected at once. In its place, we must do everything we can to build our own versions of Entropia within our local communities – in our minds, our homes, our backyards, our neighbourhoods, our suburbs, our countryside, our schools, our workplaces, our social networks, and our art – with the aim of eventually replacing growth economies with a way of life based on material sufficiency and low-energy consumption. Entropia certainly does not provide a blueprint to be applied mechanically irrespective of context, but it is an invitation – an incitation, even – to creatively adapt its lessons to varied circumstances.

As a global society that lives on a finite planet, we must embrace life beyond growth before it embraces us. It is painfully clear, however, that governments around the world are not interested in moving beyond growth, and there are few signs of things changing from the top. Empire, we can be sure, will not contemplate self-annihilation; it will struggle for existence all the way down. It follows that the revolution that is needed must emerge through an inspired and imaginative struggle 'from below'. In short, we must live the solution and show it to be good, while at the same time recognising that the great transition that is needed lies only at the end of a rough road. In the words of Theodore Roszak:

> *There is one way forward: the creation of flesh-and-blood examples of low-consumption, high-quality alternatives to the mainstream pattern of life. This we can see happening already on the*

> *counter cultural fringes. And nothing – no amount of argument or research – will take place of such living proof. What people must see is that ecologically sane, socially responsible living is good living; that simplicity, thrift, and reciprocity make for an existence that is free...*

I hesitate, however, before claiming that this approach will actually produce the just and sustainable society it promises, because most evidence suggests that people generally seem very resistant to embracing material sufficiency as a response to the problems of industrial civilisation. While transitioning toward Entropia is still an option available to us, the odds of it being selected do not look promising at all. Let us not deceive ourselves on that count. Let us also acknowledge that the transition needed will require facing up to many hard political struggles against enormously powerful forces. That is a story for another time. Nevertheless, no matter our chances of success, *trying* to build Entropia still remains the best strategy to adopt even if industrial civilisation continues to marginalise it. This is because if simpler ways of living are not embraced on a sufficiently wide scale to avoid economic or ecological collapse, those simpler ways nevertheless remain the most effective means for individuals and communities to build resilience, and in the current milieu, perhaps the ability to withstand forthcoming shocks is the best we can hope for. Entropia may be born indeed, but it may be born only on the other side of a Great Disruption. The future, however, is unwritten. We are at the crossroads and are in the process of choosing our fate.

We are the people we have been waiting for. We have to be, and if this story holds any truth, we should want to be.

Let us be pioneers once more.

ENTROPIA ECOVILLAGE

Would you be interested in helping to fund and participate in the creation of an Entropia Ecovillage outside of Melbourne, Australia, based on the ideas in this book? If so, please register your interest at www.bookofentropia.com/ecovillage. Please note, no plans have been made yet. This is purely an invitation to gauge interest and discuss feasibility.

ABOUT THE AUTHOR

Dr Samuel Alexander is a part-time lecturer with the Office for Environmental Programs, University of Melbourne, Australia. He teaches a course called 'Consumerism and the Growth Paradigm: Interdisciplinary Perspectives' in the Masters of Environment. He is also co-director of the Simplicity Institute (www.SimplicityInstitute.org) and co-founder of Transition Coburg. He writes regularly at the Simplicity Collective and posts most of his academic essays at www.TheSufficiencyEconomy.com.

Printed in Great Britain
by Amazon.co.uk, Ltd.,
Marston Gate.